Tumbleweed
Skies

Tumbleweed Skies

Valerie Sherrard

Fitzhenry & Whiteside

Text copyright © 2010 by Valerie Sherrard
Published in Canada by Fitzhenry & Whiteside,
195 Allstate Parkway, Markham, Ontario L3R 4T8

Published in the United States by Fitzhenry & Whiteside,
311 Washington Street, Brighton, Massachusetts 02135

www.fitzhenry.ca   godwit@fitzhenry.ca

10 9 8 7 6 5 4 3 2 1

National Library of Canada Cataloguing in Publication Data

Sherrard, Valerie
Tumbleweed skies / Valerie Sherrard.
ISBN 978-1-55455-113-2
I. Title.

PS8587.H3867T86 2009   jC813'.6   C2009-905581-3

Publisher Cataloging-in-Publication Data (U.S.)

Sherrard, Valerie.
Tumbleweed skies / Valerie Sherrard
[160] p. : cm.
Summary: Ellie's grandmother doesn't want her around the farm, but times
are tough, and her salesman father can't take her on the road. Ellie's challenge is
to break through her grandmother's isolation and find kinship among strangers.
ISBN: 978-1-55455-113-2 (pbk.)
1. Grandmothers — Juvenile fiction. 2. Farm life — Juvenile fiction. I. Title.
[Fic] dc22   PZ7.S547   2009

Fitzhenry & Whiteside acknowledges with thanks the Canada Council for the Arts, and
the Ontario Arts Council for their support of our publishing program. We acknowledge
the financial support of the Government of Canada through the Book Publishing
Industry Development Program (BPIDP) for our publishing activities.

Canada Council   Conseil des Arts
for the Arts   du Canada

ONTARIO ARTS COUNCIL
CONSEIL DES ARTS DE L'ONTARIO

ANCIENT FOREST™
FRIENDLY

26
trees were saved
for our forests

Preserving our environment
Fitzhenry & Whiteside chose to print the pages of this
book on recycled paper and saved these resources[1]:

	energy	water	greenhouse gases	solid waste
	8 million BTUs	45,045 L	1,121 kg	328 kg

Printed by **Webcom** Inc. on
Legacy Hi-Bulk Natural 100% post-consumer waste.

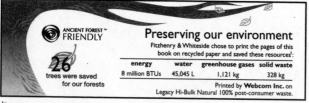

FSC

Mixed Sources
Product group from well-managed
forests, controlled sources and
recycled wood or fiber

Cert no. SW-COC-002358
www.fsc.org
© 1996 Forest Stewardship Council

[1]Estimates were made using the Environmental Defense Paper Calculator.

Design by Kong Njo
Cover illustration by David Jardine

Printed in Canada

With much love for

my beautiful granddaughters

Emilee, Ericka, and Veronicka

❖

One

I could tell right away that this wasn't a house that wanted me.

It was a bright, sunny day, but that didn't help much. The place seemed cold and unfriendly. You could tell that the outside had been painted once or twice, but years of prairie wind and sun had stripped it almost bare. And even the barn and shed and all the fields around it couldn't save the house from looking a little lost.

As we got closer, I could see that the curtains were dark and dull. The flowerbeds along the front of the house were empty, except for a few dying weeds.

Daddy slid out of the car with me right behind him, and we started toward the door. He reached out to take my hand but I pretended not to notice. I'd decided that if I had to be brave (and I'd promised

Daddy I would), I might as well start right then and there. Reaching into the pocket on my skirt, I found the brand new 1954 penny Daddy had given me. I rubbed it for luck, like my friend Judy does when she has a penny.

We walked slowly, which I hoped would give that penny enough time to work, but even so we seemed to reach the doorstep in a flash. Daddy cleared his throat and knocked. He smiled down at me.

Then the door opened and there she was. Grandmother Acklebee. She looked back and forth at us for a long minute before speaking.

"Come in," she said, but there was no welcome in her voice. She stepped back, letting out a heavy breath that made her shoulders sag inward like a balloon deflating.

"The child looks half starved," she said. She shook her head and sighed again before showing us to a dark and hazy room. A large brown couch and matching armchair were crowded into the room, along with a big clunky coffee table and end tables. It seemed that there was barely space to hold it all.

Grandma crossed the floor, her thick black shoes clunking with each step. She pulled a cord on a lamp and a dim bulb came on. It didn't do much to brighten the room.

"Sit here," she told us, pointing to the couch. She settled into the chair, adjusted herself a bit, and then looked me over like she was seeing me for the first time.

I sat and wondered if it would be all right to ask for a glass of water. Daddy had told me not to ask for anything, but maybe water would be okay. My throat was real dry from the long drive all the way from Moose Jaw. Country roads on the prairies are pretty dusty by the end of June.

I decided to wait it out for a bit. Probably, she'd offer us something before long. Most people give me milk or lemonade when I visit them with my father, and usually a snack too, like a biscuit, or brown bread and cheese, or a cookie. But when she spoke, she never said a single word about anything to eat or drink.

"So," she said, looking me over again. "I always knew it would happen one day, that you'd come begging."

"Begging!" I exclaimed. "I never even asked for a drink of water, and I'm as dry as a dust bowl."

"I was speaking," she told me, "to your father."

"Oh." How was I supposed to have known that? After all, she'd been looking at *me* while she talked. Even so, I knew I'd blurted out the wrong thing.

I thought quick and said one of the mannerly things Daddy had taught me when I was a little kid.

"I beg your pardon, ma'am." I smiled too, to show her I could be a good sport about having my thirst ignored.

She turned to my father. "So, you are not so proud now, are you?"

"I suppose not," Daddy said.

"Suppose? There is no *supposing*," she said. She crossed her arms and looked like she was waiting for something.

"No, Mrs., ah, Mother Acklebee, I don't guess there is. If you got my letter, you know why I'm here, and you know I've got nowhere else to turn. Someone's got to care for Ellie. Being kin and all, I was hoping you'd find it in your heart to take her in. Like I said in the letter, it would only be until I can get on my feet again."

Daddy had just taken a new job, traveling around and selling pots and pans for the Marvelous Cookware Company. That's the name of them and I guess they're probably marvelous all right, but I can't say for sure because we don't have a set.

"She seems a saucy sort of child," Grandma said.

"No, ma'am. She's a good girl," he told her. His face got a little red. "Sometimes she gets a bit eager, is all."

"I don't like children who speak out of turn," she said.

"Ellie knows her manners," Daddy insisted. "Don't you, Ellie?"

"Yes, sir." I knew I had to say it, to show that I really did have good manners and such because, like Daddy just said, there was nowhere else for me to go. But I sure wished I could have just up and said what I really thought, which wasn't nearly as mannerly.

"And you have *nowhere* else to go?" Grandma said.

"Nowhere," Daddy repeated. His voice was tired and quiet.

She stood up, so we did too. She looked at me for a long minute and then back at my father. She almost smiled.

"No," she said.

Two

Daddy stood there staring at her, looking helpless and beaten. I could see his jaw working, like he was chewing gum, and I thought he might say something to her, but he didn't. Instead, he picked up his hat from the coffee table and reached down with his other hand, giving me a little nudge toward the doorway.

I can't say I was sorry to go, turning down the hall and walking—head high—to the door we'd come through when we first got there. I don't know if my grandmother came behind us or not, because I never stopped or looked back.

Instead, I made a beeline for the car and hopped in—on the driver's side. The passenger door hasn't opened right since Hank Layton backed his truck into it last year. Hank told Daddy he'd pay to get it fixed as soon as he had the money. I guess he hasn't had it yet. Anyway, I crawled across the seat and plopped down in my spot.

But Daddy didn't get in after me. I turned to see why, and there he was, walking toward a man who was crossing the field, headed in our direction. The man looked to be around Daddy's age or a bit older.

They reached each other and shook hands. Then they stood there talking and talking for ages and ages. When they finally came over to the car, the stranger leaned down and peered in at me.

"Ellie, this here is your Uncle Roger," Daddy said.

I said hello and tried not to show my surprise at the way he looked. Most of him was tanned good and dark from working in the sun, but the left side of his face was all wrinkled and puckered, and as pale as a frog's belly.

"How you doin' there, Ellie?"

"Fine, thank you, sir." I made my mouth smile.

"Uncle Roger," Daddy reminded me.

"Uncle Roger," I said.

"I reckon you're wonderin' what happened to my face," Uncle Roger said.

I felt like I'd been caught doing something awful bad, and there was no way out. Daddy says it's wrong to lie, but telling the truth didn't seem the right thing to do just then either. Luckily, he didn't wait for me to answer.

"Got burned a while back, when my barn caught fire," he said. "Had to go in to save the cows."

"Yes, sir, Uncle Roger," I said.

"Got 'em all out," he told me. "But it earned me this here lifelong souvenir."

He reached up and rubbed the scar with three fingers. I was finding it hard to swallow.

"It was no big loss anyhow," he chuckled. "I never was much to look at in the first place. Now, your ma—*she* was the looker in the family."

"Yes, sir," I said. I couldn't take my eyes off the side of his face that had been burned. I could see that even though the skin was creased, it was also strangely smooth.

"You remember that your mom was your Uncle Roger's little sister," my father said.

It hadn't occurred to me one way or the other, but I nodded and finally managed to pull my eyes away from my uncle's face.

"Anyway, it was good to see you again, Roger," Daddy was saying. He began to add that we'd better get moving along, but Uncle Roger spoke up.

"Be a darned shame to head off right now. Why, it's mealtime, and 'sides that, there's nowhere to put up overnight in these parts, unless you want to put yourself at the mercy of Mrs. Minnabow and her boarding house, and I don't recommend that.

"You just wait here a minute and I'll talk to Ma. I'm sure she's just bein' stubborn. Can't see her refusin' you a meal and a place to stay, at least for a night."

Daddy agreed to wait and see, but he slid into the seat beside me just the same. Like me, I think he figured Uncle Roger was just wasting his breath. We were both surprised when he came out to the car a few minutes later and told us to come on back in and wash up for supper.

Three

I could see that Daddy had to fight to make himself get out of the car and go back into that house. I acted like I didn't notice, but I did. And I knew why he was doing it, too.

We were broke, that's why. His job at the mill had disappeared with a bunch of layoffs a while back, and he hadn't been able to find anything else for months, not until he'd signed on with the Marvelous Cookware Company.

It was temporary, he'd told me. Just until the harvest when the mill would go back to full operation. Then everything would be normal again and he wouldn't have to drag me around the countryside trying to find somewhere for me to stay while he sold his Marvelous pots and pans.

In the meantime, a meal wasn't something we

could afford to turn down. We'd been living off jam sandwiches wrapped in waxed paper since we left home, and even they were just about gone. What little money we had was needed for gas so Daddy could drive around and sell Marvelous Cookware and get us back on our feet.

So we went inside and Daddy told Grandma that we were much obliged to her. We washed our hands real good to get the dust off and waited quietly until Grandma called us to the table.

I was reaching for the glass of water in front of my plate when I felt a sharp slap on my hand.

"In *this* house," Grandma told me, "we ask the Good Lord to bless our food before we eat."

"Yes, ma'am," I said. "I'm sorry." The sight and smell of the food—boiled potatoes, beets, and pork hocks—was making my mouth water, but I bowed my head obediently.

Grandma said grace, but after that she was silent for the rest of the meal. She didn't speak or look up from her plate. You'd have thought that food was the most fascinating thing in the world, the way she studied it.

Uncle Roger just plain ignored her, talking about the weather and this and that, and acting like everything was perfectly normal.

"Got yourself an Oldsmobile, I see," Uncle Roger said to Daddy at one point.

"A '48 Futuramic," Daddy agreed. "Got a real deal on this beauty. What year's your Ford?"

"She's a '47," Uncle Roger answered, spooning more beets onto his plate. "Best pickup I ever had. Your car get good mileage?"

"Not bad," Daddy said. "I just hope gas won't go up while I'm doing this sales job. Twenty-five cents a gallon is high enough."

"We don't talk about money at the dinner table," Grandma muttered without looking up. And that was the single, solitary thing she said the whole meal.

When we'd finished eating, Daddy and Uncle Roger went outside to stretch their legs. I was left in the kitchen to help with the dishes. I picked up the drying towel and lifted the clean plates and glasses from the drain tray, doing my best not to stand too close to my grandmother.

"Your uncle," she said after we'd finished, "wants you to stay."

I felt bunches of cloth in my hands and realized I was holding onto the sides of my skirt. I'm not really a skirt kind of girl, but Daddy said I should wear it to meet my relations.

"Stop that fidgeting," Grandma said.

"Yes, ma'am," I said and unclenched my fists, letting the orange and brown plaid folds fall back into place.

"You will help out in the house and do what you are told. There will be no saucy talk, no noise, and no touching things that do not belong to you. We eat at mealtimes only. You will not help yourself to anything or go into the fridge. You will make your bed properly every morning."

"Yes, ma'am," I said. I tried to smile but it was hard because there were tears trying to fill up my eyes.

"I will give you this one chance and that's all," she said.

I wanted to tell her that I didn't want her stupid chance, that I'd rather sleep in the trunk of Daddy's car and live on jam sandwiches for the rest of the summer than be in her mean, dark house. But I couldn't.

"Yes, ma'am," I said. "Thank you, Grandma."

The look on Grandma's face might have made me laugh, except *I* was even more surprised to hear the word *Grandma* coming out of my mouth than she was. She didn't say anything, though. Instead, she went to the back door and called out for Uncle Roger.

Before he got there, Grandma sent me down the hall. I wasn't sure where to go when I got to the end, so I just stood off to the side, out of sight. It wasn't on purpose, but it turned out that I could hear their conversation pretty clearly from there.

"I think this is a mistake," Grandma told Uncle Roger, "but since you're so set on it, I've decided to let the child stay."

"I'm glad," Uncle Roger said. "She's Maggie's girl, Ma. We owe it to her."

"We owe nothing."

"Well, it'll be nice anyway, having a little one around."

"Humph," Grandma said, "I know one thing. I raised my family without shoving my children off on anyone else. An old woman needs her peace."

I was hoping Daddy would stay at Grandma's too, at least for the first night, but he didn't. He said he was too restless to sleep, and he meant to drive right through the night, clear across Saskatchewan to his territory.

I asked him to show it to me, even though he'd already done that twice before. Daddy took out the map and unfolded it on the hood of the car.

"Now, where's Saskatchewan?" he asked. I pointed to it and he nodded.

"My territory is this triangle of land right here, smack dab on the Alberta border," he said, tracing his finger from Battleford to Meadow Lake to Lloydminster.

"But what if you get lost there?" I asked.

"No need to worry about that," Daddy said. "I'll have my map with me the whole time. Now, you be a good girl and listen to your grandma while I'm gone. Do what she tells you and I'll be back for you as soon as I can."

I said goodbye and I didn't even cry…but he was still right there in front of me then. Just saying words like *goodbye* isn't the same as seeing a car drive away, its back to you, getting farther and farther until you can't even see the puff of dust behind it.

Four

I woke up the next morning with a thought already coming into my head, and that thought was *I'm in a strange place*. For one thing, as soon as I opened my eyes I could see that I was looking at the wrong ceiling. There was no round white light in the middle; this ceiling was dingy and yellowed, with a big, dark-edged stain in one spot.

As I stared up, a feeling came over me like I might have to cry. But I held it back. Twice, I closed my eyes and opened them again, but nothing had changed. Slowly I let my eyes wander around the room, taking in the faded wallpaper, the dark, bulky dresser, the window, and the door.

At home, the window is over my bed. I like to start out every morning by standing up on my bed and pressing my nose against the glass. That way, I can see right off what kind of show the new day is putting on.

In this room, the window was on the wall to my right and it wasn't that high up. I guessed I could go look out if I wanted, even though I knew I wasn't going to see the green fence and the top of the shed next door, like I would have seen from my room at home.

I got out of bed and crossed to the window expecting nothing but a plain old field and barn. They were there, all right, but there was something else, too, and it was moving. It was a dark golden color, and as I got focused on it I could see that it was a dog. Only, there was something wrong with its head—at least I thought there was at first.

Then I realized why it didn't look right. That dog had a bird in its mouth! Without pausing for one second, I yanked open the bedroom door, pounded down the stairs, and charged down the hall, through the kitchen, and out the back door, yelling, "NOOOOOOOOOOO!" the whole way.

That dumb dog got to the yard just as I did. I must have startled him because he opened his mouth and dropped the bird lickety-split.

"Bad!" I yelled. "Go away!" I hurried to the bird and picked it up, my heart bursting with sorrow. It looked like I was going to have to put on a funeral, like Judy and I did the time her hamster got loose and met up with the wrong cat.

The bird was black and white with a blue shine in its dark feathers. It lay very still in my hands. I couldn't help myself; I started to cry. I was trying to think through what kind of funeral I could have for this bird, seeing as how I'd never even met it before that very moment, when I heard someone behind me.

"Ellie?" It was Uncle Roger.

"That dog killed this bird for no good reason," I told him. I hoped he understood from my tone that if that dog was his, he might want to have a word with it.

Uncle Roger stepped forward and squatted down in front of me. He looked the bird over, and while he was doing that I felt something move.

"It's alive!" I gasped, almost dropping it in surprise.

"Yep," Uncle Roger said. "And by the way, that was our neighbor's dog, Bailey. He's a nice fella, really. I'm sure he was just playing. He wouldn't have meant any harm to the bird—which is a magpie, by the way."

"Is it going to be all right?" I asked. I didn't bother to tell him that he was wasting his time trying to improve my opinion of that murdering fleabag of a neighbor's dog.

"Let's take it in the back porch and have a closer look," Uncle Roger said. "And be ready to tell your grandmother you're sorry for running through her house hollering a moment ago. She's not much used to that sort of thing and I don't reckon she'll be taking it well."

Uncle Roger was right about Grandma. She was standing in the middle of the kitchen with her arms crossed over her chest and her eyes blazing. I could see that she was about to lecture me so I spoke up quick.

"I'm awful sorry for yelling and running through the house," I told her. "But this bird was in a dog's mouth! And I rescued it. Now we're going to see if it's okay."

"You don't yell in my house again," Grandma said. She glanced at the magpie. "And no birds in here!"

"Don't worry, we're just taking a quick look," Uncle Roger said. Grandma turned away.

Uncle Roger put the bird down very carefully, sitting it on its feet before he started to examine it. It didn't take long to realize that one of the wings looked different than the other. I watched, hardly daring to breathe as he checked them.

"Well, it doesn't seem to be broken, so I guess it's some other kind of injury," he said. "A sprain maybe, or bruising. But the bird won't be able to fly until it's healed, which leaves it pretty defenseless."

"I'll take care of it until then!" I cried. "We can't let it die."

"I reckon there's a cage out in the shed that you could keep it in," Uncle Roger said slowly. "But you'll have to feed it."

I jumped up and down and clapped. "I will! I will!" I promised. "But what will we name it? Is it a boy or a girl?"

"It's hard to tell with magpies," Uncle Roger said. He put his hands around the bird and lifted it gently, holding it securely against his chest. "Right now it needs to be bandaged up more than it needs a name."

I thought a bandage would be a bit small to help this magpie's wing, but I didn't say so. I followed Uncle Roger to the barn and was surprised when he rummaged around in an old flour sack and came up with a long, white strip of cloth.

"This should do it," he said. He wrapped the cloth around the magpie's injured wing and body, so that the only part that wasn't wrapped was the good wing. He sewed the end closed with a big needle and some kind of string.

All the while that this was going on, the magpie just stared, but as Uncle Roger finished tying off the string it let out a squawk.

"Ree!" it cried. *"Ree! Ree!"*

"All that racket is a good sign if I ever saw one," Uncle Roger said.

"I guess," I said. "It sure isn't going to win any singing contests, though, that's for sure."

"Magpies aren't exactly songbirds," he agreed with a chuckle. "But by the sound of it, at least this one is going to be okay."

"But I still don't know what to call it," I said with a sigh. "Are you sure you can't tell if it's a boy or girl?"

"If I *had* to pick one, I'd say it was a boy. To be on the safe side, why don't you call it something that goes good for either one?" Uncle Roger suggested.

"Like what?"

"Well, Sammy for instance. Sammy can be short for Samuel or Samantha."

I looked at the bird and then back at Uncle Roger. I felt a smile showing up on my face. "That's perfect, Uncle Roger!" I said. "Sammy is a *perfect* name for this bird."

"But now don't get too attached," Uncle Roger said. "Soon's it can fly again, it'll be gone."

All day long I couldn't stop thinking about Sammy. Every chance I had, I snuck off to the shed and checked up on him. It helped me steer clear of Grandma too, since she stayed in a grumpy mood all day. At least, I hoped it was a grumpy mood and not her regular, everyday way of acting.

Uncle Roger and I spent most of that evening hunting up food for Sammy. We dug up a few earthworms and gathered together a disgusting collection of flies, beetles, and other bugs.

"Magpies are carrion eaters too," Uncle Roger told me.

"Are there any of those around here?" I asked.

"*Carrion* is just a word for animals that are dead," Uncle Roger explained. "Sometimes I find dead moles and mice and such in the field. Sammy would eat things like that, too."

I stared at him, horrified. Bugs and worms were bad enough, but picking up dead old rodents was more than I could stand.

"Maybe you'd rather just feed Sammy worms and bugs," he said quickly.

The bugs were all dead. Uncle Roger gave me the cover from an old Eaton's catalogue to slide under them after we killed them. Once they were on it, I lifted them up and dumped them into a small jar without touching them. That was especially helpful for the ones that got squished. They looked dry and hard and much smaller than when they'd been alive.

I would have preferred to let Uncle Roger take care of picking them up, but he said I might just as well learn how to do it myself, because he wasn't going to have time to be scrounging up food for a bird every day.

The worms, on the other hand, were alive in a big jar of earth. Uncle Roger punched some tiny holes in the lid with a hammer and nail, so there'd be enough air, though I didn't see why anything that lived in dirt needed air.

When we'd finished collecting food for Sammy, Uncle Roger double-checked that the cage was good and secure. "Seems solid," he told me, "but when you come in here in the morning, just open the door a crack at first and peek through to make sure that Sammy is in his cage."

"Do you think he could get out?" I asked.

"It's not likely, but you never know. Now, I've got a few things to do before my day's work is done. You run along inside and get ready for bed."

I went in quietly, hoping to avoid Grandma. But, when I opened the door into the kitchen, I saw her sitting at the table. Her back was to me and she was shaking her head.

"I told her," I heard Grandma say. "I *told* her not to go to that dance."

Five

I was born on June 4th, 1944, which is also the day my mother died. Since I never got to know her, it might seem strange that I miss her. But sometimes I really do.

Daddy talks about her a lot. It almost seems that his stories have turned into memories to me. I look at her picture and can practically *see* the things he's told me about. Things like the way she covered her mouth with her hand when she giggled and how she liked wildflowers better than the ones they sell in flower shops. She hummed songs when she was cleaning house and wore white gloves to church every Sunday.

My mother's eyes were blue and they smiled a lot, unless she saw a person or animal that was hurt. Then they filled with tears and her bottom lip trembled, because she had a big heart for anything that was suffering.

Daddy's told me the story of how they met so many times I could have told it myself. I never did, though. I just kept asking him to tell it again.

"She was like a vision," he'd say. His arm would snake around me and he'd tug me over and kind of tuck me under his arm. He'd smile down at me, but then his eyes always moved off to the day he was talking about.

"I met her in '42. It was just after the third time I tried to join the army and couldn't get in on account of my eyesight. I was angry at that time—angry that I couldn't serve my country the way a man ought to. Most of my friends had enlisted and I couldn't stand being in the old neighborhood. It set me on the road, kind of drifting around the countryside. Next thing I knew, I was harvesting near Weybolt. One Saturday evening I found myself at a barn dance there."

I would sit up straighter and listen hard when he got to that part. Because my mother was next.

"She was there that night. Pretty as a picture, your mother. First time I laid eyes on her, I knew she was the girl for me."

He and my mother had met at that dance and fallen in love. When Daddy moved on, the only thing he thought about was finding a good job so he could marry her.

He wrote to her every week, only she didn't answer his letters. That didn't stop him though! Once he got his job at the mill, he just headed right up there to Weybolt and went straight to her house.

When he knocked on the door, Grandma answered and told him my mom didn't want to see him. She sent him away. Daddy drove out the gateway and onto the road feeling like he'd taken the flat side of a shovel right in the stomach. But then he saw my mother standing on the side of the road, waving for him to stop. She'd heard what had happened at the door, and had snuck out and run to the road to meet him.

While they drove along talking, my mom told him that she'd never received any of his letters. That's why she hadn't written back. But she still loved him too.

And then my father realized she'd put herself in a bad spot, running off that way. The only solution was for them to get married right quick, which they did.

My mom wrote to her family, but her parents never answered that letter or any of the others she wrote over the next year. Not once. Only her brother Roger wrote back. One time, he even came to visit for a few days.

Then I came along. But there were problems, and my mom died shortly after giving birth to me. Daddy says she saw me, though, and even in that short time she had with me, she loved me with her whole heart.

He sent a telegram to her family with the terrible news. They arrived the same day and took over the arrangements. They wanted my mother to be sent back to Weybolt to be buried. My grandmother insisted it was their right because they'd had her for her whole life until he came and took her away. And, she told him, look what happened then.

My father didn't have any fight in him, because of being heartbroken and all. He just let Grandma do what she wanted.

Over the years he wrote them once in a while and sent some pictures of me. Now and then he got back a note from Roger, but there was never anything from my grandparents. Then, when I was three, my grandfather died. The only time he'd ever seen me was when I was just born.

Since I knew the whole story, I understood right away what Grandma meant that evening when I went into the kitchen and found her at the table muttering, "I told her not to go to that dance. I told her no good would come of it."

I stood real still, hardly daring to breathe. It didn't matter. Grandma turned after a moment and saw me there. Then she said something horrible.

"You and your father," she said, "you killed her, the two of you."

I couldn't believe anyone could say such an awful thing. It made me want to hit her, even if she was my grandmother. I wanted to clench my hands into hard, tight fists and pound on her until she took it back.

Words rushed into my head—loud, angry words—but they wouldn't come out of my mouth. That was good, because if I'd said what I was thinking, Grandma would most likely have thrown me out, and I would have had nowhere to go.

The worst thing was I'd wondered that very thing before. I'd even asked Daddy, but he swore that wasn't the case. He said that it had been Momma's time to die and that because of me she was able to die happy.

But what if Grandma was right? I didn't think I could bear that.

Six

It took all the courage I had to go downstairs the next morning. I paused on every single step and hoped and wished for Uncle Roger to be there in the kitchen. But when I got to the end of the hall I saw that Grandma was alone at the table.

My legs felt like they were going to turn around and run back upstairs all on their own—and they might have too, except Grandma spoke up.

"Your porridge is getting cold." She nodded toward a bowl on the table. "Come and eat."

I made my way obediently to the table and hoisted myself onto the wooden chair nearest the bowl.

"Thank you, Grandma," I said. I almost knocked my breakfast over when my spoon skidded through the milk and across the rubbery surface of the porridge, and banged against the edge of the dish.

Catching it in time, I tried again more firmly and brought a lukewarm glob to my mouth.

When Daddy makes porridge it's hot and sweet and delicious. This was hardly lukewarm and there was barely a hint of brown sugar. I didn't care. Eating gave me something to do, something to look at, and I went about it as slowly as I could.

Grandma sat there until I was about halfway through, and then she got up and crossed over to the sink. She poured hot water from the kettle into an enamel basin, added a few dippers of cold from the bucket under the pump, and started washing the breakfast dishes.

I gulped down the rest of my porridge and hurried over with my bowl. I picked up the towel and began to dry the dishes that were already piling up in the drain tray. It was a relief when the last thing was dried and put away and Grandma told me to find something to do outside until it was time for lunch chores. I was only too glad to escape out to the shed—and Sammy.

"Ree! Ree! Ree!" he screeched the second I stepped into the shed. He might have had a bruised wing, but I can tell you that his voice was strong enough! It sounded like the sharp, creaky sound of a door hinge squeaking.

"I don't speak Magpie," I told him, "so you might as well settle down."

Sammy tilted his head to one side and stared at me crossly. His dark eyes seemed to say that he didn't think much of my comment.

"REE!" he squawked even louder. *"REE! REE! REE!"*

"Yelling isn't going to do you any good," I told him. I gave him a stern look right back, which just set him off again.

"I'm saving your life, you know," I told him. "You'd get gobbled up first thing if you were free."

Sammy's head bobbed up and down a couple of times, like he was agreeing with me. That made me laugh, which seemed to interest him. His dark little eyes watched me closely.

"That's more like it," I said. "And don't forget that I'm the one feeding you, so you'd better be nice to me."

"Ree! Ree!" he answered. Actually, I'm not *sure* he was answering, but it kind of looked that way.

I unscrewed the lid from the jar we'd put the worms in and hauled a long skinny one out of the dirt. It dangled for a second or two and then started to scrunch in on itself, getting shorter and shorter. I dropped it into the cage. Sammy hopped over to inspect it. As soon as he tilted himself down to start eating it, I turned and hurried out of the shed.

I guess it was silly, but I felt guilty about that worm. It didn't even help to tell myself that if Sammy had been out on his own, he'd have been gobbling down worms left and right. I was the one who'd dug that worm up and handed it over to be eaten.

I kicked around the backyard for a bit, trying not to think about it. That was a lot harder than I expected. Before long, I was even imagining that worm had a sad, worried look on his face when I dropped him into Sammy's cage, as if he'd known he was being sacrificed.

Why do I *have to die so this bird can live?* the worm in my head was wondering.

It bothered me until I made up my mind to go back in there and rescue that worm—if it wasn't already too late. But just as I was turning to go back into the shed, a big black car came lumbering into the driveway.

The car itself wasn't particularly interesting, except that it seemed to be driving itself.

That got my attention.

Forgetting all about the worm (which was probably in Sammy's tummy by then anyway), I hurried toward the car.

I stopped and stood still as soon as I reached the front corner of the house. There was no sense in crowding a driverless car.

The door began to swing open. I took a couple of steps back. My heart beat harder. Then feet and legs appeared and, as the door closed, their owner came into view.

It was the tiniest man I'd ever seen. He was only a little taller than me, and last month, when Daddy made a new mark on the doorway at home, I was four feet four inches. He put me in mind at once of a little elf, with bright, shiny eyes, a pink mouth and cheeks, and a sharply pointed nose. His eyebrows arched like upside-down Vs, although that might have been because he was surprised to find me standing there. "How do, ma'am!" he said. His voice was odd, too—squeaky but grown up at the same time. "Are you the new lady of the house?"

"No, sir," I told him, even though I could see he was teasing. "My grandma is."

"Your *grandma*?" His eyes grew rounder and bugged out.

"Yes, sir. My Grandmother Acklebee."

He shook his head and then slapped it as if he was trying to wake himself up.

"Mr. Cobb." Grandma spoke from the doorway, where she'd appeared.

"Mornin', Mizz Acklebee, ma'am." Mr. Cobb swept one arm out to the side and bowed at the waist. "I was just making the acquaintance of your—"

"Come in," Grandma told him.

"Why, thank you kindly." Mr. Cobb scampered to the back door of the car. He yanked it open, lunged inside, and reappeared almost instantly lugging a large, black satchel. It was leather—old and cracked and so full that it was straining at the seams.

Mr. Cobb made no further attempt at conversation while he carried the bag inside. It seemed that the task of lifting it took all the strength he had and some besides.

Even after he'd gotten seated in the kitchen, it took a moment for Mr. Cobb to stop huffing and gasping. When his breathing finally evened out, he smiled secretively and reached for his satchel.

Seven

M r. Cobb placed the bag on an empty chair and arranged it at his side. He opened the mouth of it just a little and peeked down into its depths. With slow, deliberate movements, he began to lift things out of it one at a time.

Grandma Acklebee leaned forward. Her whole attention was concentrated on whatever was in that bag.

Mr. Cobb drew out a shiny silver eggbeater with a red wooden handle and knob. He turned the knob quickly and the beaters became a blur.

"Very popular, this item," he said. "You can make meringue in no time with this beater."

"I have a beater," Grandma said. She waved it away and Mr. Cobb laid it off to one side on the table and reached in for the next item.

He brought out a can opener, a rolling pin, trivets,

a glass reamer, a knife sharpener, a can opener and a flour sifter. Mr. Cobb talked about each thing for a minute before Grandma cut him off and decided against it.

I was almost ready to give up on there being anything tempting in the bag when he pulled out a box that was full of cookie cutters in all different shapes. I looked at the picture on the box with interest. There was a heart and a star and a Christmas tree, which made sense. I wasn't quite so sure about the turkey or some of the other animals, but the one that really seemed strange was the fish. Who would want to make cookies shaped like fish?

Not Grandma, it seemed. She passed on the cookie cutters too.

"Now here's a nice everyday butter mould," Mr. Cobb said cheerfully. He didn't seem discouraged that Grandma kept turning everything down. "Look at the workmanship of the finger joints on each and every corner."

Grandma actually took the mould and turned it around a few times. She inspected the wooden knob and the corners. Then she shook her head and gave it back.

"Not too many ladies can resist this next item," Mr. Cobb announced. He paused, to build suspense I suppose, before pulling out a strange looking gadget shaped rather like a can opener. He held it up for us to admire.

"This combination tool does so many things I hope I can remember them all," Mr. Cobb announced. "Why, it opens jars and bottles, tenderizes meat, and even pits cherries. And if that wasn't enough, it's also a garlic press."

Grandma looked this gadget over too and put it on the table beside her without saying anything. Next, Mr. Cobb showed her a pasta cutter and a pie-crust edger and a spice grater. She left them all near her on the table.

"Here's another very popular item this season," the salesman told her, pulling out a chimney flue cover with a winter scene on it. "In fact, I don't think I have but two or three of them left all told."

"There's nothing wrong with my flue cover," Grandma said. "Anyway, black is more practical."

Mr. Cobb nodded and put his aside. And then he smiled his thin smile and pulled out a pink and yellow cardboard box, rectangular shaped. He admired it for a second before turning it around so that the cellophane window faced Grandma and me.

It was a doll. It had brown hair and blue eyes, and it was dressed in a yellow dress and matching hat.

The smile on Mr. Cobb's face grew wider, which stretched his lips even thinner. "This doll," he said, "is mighty popular with the little ladies. It sure is. And a bargain at only one dollar and ninety cents. Dolls like this are selling for three dollars or more in the stores, and if you want my opinion they're not nearly as nice as this one. Why, I'll just bet this is the finest doll you've ever seen."

Suddenly my chest hurt, and not because I wanted that doll. I didn't—not even a little bit. It hurt because I could see anger on Grandma's face. Even though I hadn't caused it, I felt as guilty and ashamed as if I'd been begging her to buy that doll for me.

Mr. Cobb leaned toward me, holding the hateful thing out. "Would you like to hold it?" he asked, winking at me.

"No, sir." I said. "No, thank you."

Grandma's chin lifted a little.

Mr. Cobb looked confused. He drew the doll back and looked it over as if he was trying to figure out what was wrong with it.

"I've seen enough for today," Grandma said.

"Oh?" Mr. Cobb said. His eyebrows rushed together in a frown. "But I haven't shown you—"

"It's enough," Grandma repeated. Very deliberately she pushed the pastry edger and pasta cutter back across the table to Mr. Cobb. Then she nodded at the two remaining items. "I will take just these—the garlic press and spice grater. How much do I owe you?"

Mr. Cobb gave her a price and she paid him. As small as he already was, he seemed to shrink a little. He gathered up his wares and put them back into the black bag, leaving out only the two things Grandma had purchased.

"Now, I'll try to get back before the snow flies but I can't make any promises," Mr. Cobb told her as he tucked away the last few things. "I sure hope there's nothing you'll need before my next visit."

"Anything I managed without for all these years, I can manage without until you come again," Grandma said.

And then he was gone, struggling to carry his bag back the way he'd come. Grandma saw him to the door but not before she gave me a look that made it clear I was to stay right where I was.

When she returned to the kitchen, she picked up her new gadgets, looked them over again, washed them, and put them into a drawer.

Eight

The next day was Saturday. Right after breakfast was over and I'd given Sammy his morning meal, Grandma announced that we would be going to town. She looked me up and down with one of her sighs and said that I should put on something that made me look like less of a ragamuffin. To that, she added that I might *try* to behave myself properly and not disgrace her in front of other people.

I put on the skirt I'd worn that first day and brushed my hair extra carefully. I even turned one of my white ankle socks inside out and used it to shine up my patent leather shoes before putting them on. Even though I was going with Grandma, the thought of a trip into Weybolt was exciting. It would be my first chance to see the town that had been my mother's for her whole life—or, at least until she married my dad. I wanted to look my best.

But when I presented myself downstairs, Grandma shook her head sadly like she just couldn't quite believe what she saw.

"Come, sit," she said, pointing to a chair.

I went nervously and was startled when she began yanking at my hair. For a second I thought she was pulling at it for no reason, but I soon realized she was making braids.

"Hold still!" she told me more than once.

I did my best, even though it was difficult with Grandma tugging and jerking my head the whole time. When she was finished, she said she was no miracle worker and that was the best she could do.

I'd never had braids before. I can only make ponytails. It would have been nice to see how the braids looked, but there was no chance for that. Grandma shooed me into the middle of the seat of Uncle Roger's truck and told me not to be making noise on the drive. Then she got in beside me—on the passenger side.

"Is Uncle Roger coming too?" I asked.

"Of course he is," Grandma said. "How else would we get there?"

"I thought you were going to drive," I told her.

"I don't drive," Grandma said.

"Don't you know how?" I asked, but Grandma said nothing more.

Uncle Roger came along after another moment or two. He got in and looked down at me like he was going to say something, only he didn't. Instead he stared for a few seconds and then he faced forward and turned the key. The truck grumbled a couple of times and then started up. The motor made a low, growly sound all the way to town. It was the only sound on the whole drive—nothing like when I go in the car with Daddy. We always sing or talk or play games, like guessing which color the next car we meet will be.

I sat and watched out the window, but there wasn't much to see except more farms until we got to Weybolt. The farms all looked the same—fields and fields of grain stretching out on every side of tired-looking farmhouses. It might have been my imagination, but it seemed like the barns and silos were better cared for than the houses. Most places had big old trucks like Uncle Roger's, though I don't know if they were Ford Pickups too. They all look alike to me, with their fat fenders and wide grills like a great big smile. None of the trucks were shiny. Not like in Moose Jaw, where it seems all the men are forever washing their cars. Daddy, too. He keeps our car good and shiny all right, and he lets me help wash it and rub in the wax when it's dry, too.

First thing I saw when we reached the town was the water tower—an enormous tank held up with skinny legs. It put me in mind of a spider, the kind with a big fat body, carried around on legs that aren't much thicker than a strand of hair.

The stores in town were mostly tall wood buildings along one street. It looked like their owners had given up on painting the buildings, and the signs hanging out front or over the doors were faded too. Even the windows looked hazy and uncared for.

Uncle Roger pulled the truck to a stop beside a big, faded, olive-colored building with a sign that said Fletcher's General Store. Grandma looked down at me, like she was checking to see if I was still there. Then she sighed and told me to come along and remember to mind my Ps and Qs.

I walked through the store with her, wishing I could stop whenever there were particularly interesting things to see or smells to identify. I'm good at figuring out different smells, but there wasn't much time for any except the easy ones, like cloves and peppermint and leather.

The floor was made of long strips of wood that

lifted here and dipped there along paths worn by the customers' feet. Grandma clomped along the floor as she clutched a list tightly in one hand. She glanced at the list from time to time, adding things to her basket or sometimes just picking something up and looking it over before putting it back on the shelf. When she'd finished we went to the counter, where a thin man stood smiling.

"Good morning, Mrs. Acklebee," he said, lifting items out of her basket. "I see you have a little visitor with you today."

"I need five pounds of sugar," Grandma said, ignoring his remark, "fifty pounds of flour, a jug of molasses, and a gallon of vinegar."

He nodded, glancing at me quickly with a half smile, like he wanted to be friendly but was afraid to. He fetched the heavier items Grandma had requested.

"Is that everything for you today, then?" he asked. His voice sounded too loud and cheery. When Grandma nodded, he pulled out a book and flipped a few pages until he came to one with her name on it. He wrote down each thing in the order and added up the total. Then he turned it around and slid it across the counter to Grandma.

She read it through carefully, checked his addition twice, and signed it.

He closed the book and put it under the counter, then came around to help carry the flour and other heavy things out to the car. But before the man could leave the store, Uncle Roger showed up from wherever he'd been and took the load from him.

"This is my niece, Ellie," he said as he hoisted the flour onto a broad shoulder. "Ellie, this is Wendell Fletcher."

"Pleased to meet you, Ellie," Wendell said. He smiled and shook my hand, then reached into one of the big jars of candy. "Say, do you like peppermint sticks?"

"Yes, sir, Mr. Fletcher," I said. My mouth was already starting to water.

"On the house," he said passing one to me. "Welcome to Weybolt."

I thanked him, and then he and Uncle Roger talked for a couple of minutes. After that we went back to the car, where Grandma was sitting, hands folded on her lap, looking straight ahead.

Nine

One thing I can say for Grandma—she's good at braiding hair. Even though we drove to town and back with the windows down and the air blowing through the car, the braids were still in good shape when I finally got to see them.

After a long look in the bathroom mirror, I decided I didn't care for them. They were smooth and even, but it felt strange to have my hair tamed that way. It's always been kind of wild—long, brown waves dancing around my head. Even tied with rubber bands, my hair is quite bouncy.

There was no problem with taking the braids out that night because it was Saturday, which of course meant a bath. I washed myself and then scrubbed my hair and rinsed it slowly with a jug of warm water.

The water felt nice running over my shoulders and down into the big round wooden tub.

Just sitting in the water felt good, but there was no time to relax and enjoy it because Uncle Roger still had to have his turn and it was already starting to cool.

I squeezed my hair to get some of the water out, wrapped a stiff white towel around me, and stepped onto the back porch floor. After a quick towel-off, I slipped my cotton nightie over my head and went inside to get my comb.

"Did you wash your ears?" Grandma asked. She'd bathed first and had already combed her hair and put it back into the tight bun she wore.

"Yes'm," I said, though it wasn't true. I soothed my conscience by deciding they'd probably gotten clean when I was washing my hair.

Grandma didn't check. Instead, she said it was bedtime and I should say my prayers with extra care because tomorrow was the Lord's Day and it would be a terrible thing for me to go to the Lord's House with my heart all black and sinful.

"Yes, Grandma," I said. "Good night, Grandma."

"Just mind what I told you," she said.

I made sure to kneel beside my bed for my prayers that night. I usually do that anyway—at least,

I do most of the time, but sometimes I forget until I'm already in bed under the blankets feeling good and sleepy. When that happens it's hard to get back out so I usually just sit up and clasp my hands together and hope God doesn't mind.

When I'd finished owning up to fibbing about washing my ears and having unkind thoughts about my grandmother, I got to the "God blesses." I always say God bless Daddy and my friends Sheila and Judy. Then I do Ron and Yvonne Laughlin, who are our neighbors back in Moose Jaw, and Premier Douglas and Prime Minister St. Laurent (because Daddy says we're supposed to pray for our country's leader, even if he is a Liberal).

I was about to say *Amen* and jump into bed when it struck me that I should probably be adding on Grandma and Uncle Roger. I didn't mind Uncle Roger, but I was kind of grudging asking God to bless Grandma. After I'd finished up and gotten under the covers, I wondered if maybe I'd gone and blackened my heart again, so I got back out of bed and back on my knees.

"P.S.," I said, "If it was a sin to ask You to bless Grandma when I didn't really mean it, could You go ahead and forgive that, too?"

That must have done the trick, because I slept peaceful as can be and woke up in the morning feeling just a tiny bit less homesick.

I expected we'd be going to church in Weybolt so I was surprised that Uncle Roger headed his truck the other way.

Like most tall buildings on the prairies, the church came into view long before we reached it. It stood out against the sky, tall and thin and white. I listened hard, hoping it had a bell, but there was only silence.

Grandma said she hoped she didn't have to tell me how to behave in the Lord's House and I told her no, ma'am—that I went with my daddy every Sunday. She sniffed like she doubted it, but she didn't say anything else.

In we went and sat in an empty pew four rows from the front on the left side. There were only about thirty other people there. A few of them nodded and murmured good morning, and then the preacher came out and everyone fell silent.

He preached about being a faithful witness in four ways—discipleship and stewardship and two more. I can't remember the others exactly. I don't think they were *ships*, which kind of threw me off after the first two.

When we were leaving, Uncle Roger shook the preacher's hand and introduced me to him. Grandma told him it was a good sermon and she hoped certain people were paying attention. That made me a mite nervous in case she meant me and planned to ask me questions on the way home.

Just as we reached the car, though, a girl came running over. She stopped dead in front of me and put her hands on her hips.

"I'm Marcy Knowles and I live on the third farm south of where you're staying," she said in a quick burst of words. "You can come over and play if you want to tomorrow. I have a tire swing and a real live carriage big enough to hold four dolls."

"Marcy," a woman's voice called behind her, "remember your manners."

"Yes, Momma. Good day, Mrs. Acklebee," Marcy said. She turned to face my grandmother and it seemed as if she was about to curtsey. If she meant to, she changed her mind and just looked back at me again.

"Elizabeth is busy during the day," Grandma told her. I tried not to frown when I heard that. It was true Grandma had been finding more chores for me to do each day, but it wasn't as if she really needed me. After all, she'd done everything on her own up until I got there.

"She's not so busy that she can't make new friends," Uncle Roger said just as Grandma opened her mouth to continue. "And you come along over to our place too, anytime you like, Marcy. We'd be glad to have you."

The next thing I knew, Uncle Roger had gone to talk to Marcy's mother to see what time I was to go there. Grandma looked angry, but she never said a word. She just got into the truck and sat there as usual—stiff and still as a rock.

When we got back to the farm I hurried out to tell Sammy about the invitation. You'd think he might have shown some sign of being glad for me, since I was his only friend at the moment, but all he did was scream for some bugs and add another dropping to the paper lining his cage.

Ten

"**A**t the very least, *try* to remember that you're a girl."

This was Grandma's last instruction to me before Uncle Roger delivered me over to Marcy's place the next morning. It came at the end of a short speech about minding my Ps and Qs and not disgracing the family name (though I don't know how I could do much harm to the Acklebee name since my last name is Stewart) and not giving Mrs. Knowles any trouble.

I just kept saying, "Yes, ma'am," until she was finished. For once her crabbiness wasn't bothering me a bit. I was escaping, even if it was only for a few hours.

Marcy was waiting on her porch when we drove up the lane to her house. As soon as I saw her, I was thankful that Grandma had made me put on a skirt.

Marcy was wearing a red and white polka-dot dress with matching red shoes.

I told Uncle Roger thank you very much, and scooted out of the car.

"We're going to have perogies and iced cakes for lunch," Marcy declared, bouncing down the steps with a doll under one arm. "And mother says you can sleep over some night and we can stay up to listen to the radio until nine-thirty!"

My father lets me stay up past ten sometimes, but Marcy seemed so impressed with her announcement that I thought it would be rude to spoil it for her. Besides, I couldn't imagine Grandma letting me stay for a whole night.

"So, what do you want to play first? We could play mother and father and baby—only you'll have to be the father. Last Christmas I was supposed to be a shepherd in the school play, only mother told Miss Walashyn that I couldn't because my features are too delicate and dainty for a male part. We have a lot more girls in class than boys, so some girls had to take boy parts, you see. But I ended up as an angel and mother said I looked *and* acted the part."

Marcy looped an arm with mine and held up her doll with her free hand. "This is Molly. Her dress is real velvet."

I touched Molly's dress, which was smooth and soft.

"You want to hold her?" Marcy offered. "Just for a minute, though, because she's new. I got her for my birthday in April when I turned ten."

I took Molly and held her for a few seconds. By then Marcy was already looking kind of nervous, so I passed the doll back. I really didn't mind because I've never much liked hard plastic dolls, and that was even truer since Mr. Cobb had tried to get Grandma to buy me one. I have a Raggedy Ann and she might not be pretty like Molly, but she's soft and cuddly and she suits me.

Marcy and I played house for a while but it wasn't that much fun being the husband.

"Maybe we can be sisters, and the baby can be our niece," I suggested after a few moments.

"No, this is better," Marcy insisted. Then she frowned. "You keep forgetting to make your voice deep—like a man's."

"Sorry," I said, but the look on Marcy's face made me realize that I'd apologized in my regular girl voice. "I mean, *sorry*," I repeated gruffly.

But Marcy was still frowning. "I'm waiting for you to pull out my chair so I can sit down," she said. "You aren't a very good husband."

"Well, I don't really know the husband rules," I pointed out.

"Your *voice*!" Marcy folded her arms in front of her and shook her head. "Never mind. We'll pretend you have a sore throat and you can't talk."

I did my best to keep up with her orders, but after a little while even she grew bored with the one-sided conversation.

"My gracious," she said, shaking her head, "I surely hope when I grow up and have a real husband, he listens better than you do."

And I hope your husband likes having a bossy wife, I thought, but I didn't say anything out loud.

Marcy decided it was time to do something else, so we drew some pictures and colored them.

"I know! We'll both draw the same thing, and then my mother can judge whose picture is better when we're finished," Marcy said. "Let's draw rainbows. Daddy says I'm really good at drawing rainbows."

"Well, *I'm* good at drawing flowers," I said, "so that's what I'm going to draw." I picked up a red crayon and formed the bowl of a tulip.

"No. It has to be the *same* thing," Marcy insisted, but I kept right on drawing my flowers. After a moment she let out a big noisy breath and said,

"Fine. We'll both draw two pictures—one of rainbows and one of flowers."

"Okay," I agreed. Then there was peace and quiet for a while as we worked on our drawings. When they were finished, we got Marcy's mom to judge.

Mrs. Knowles decided that Marcy's rainbow was better than mine, but my flowers were the best. She gave us each a cookie as our prize.

We had two games of Chinese checkers after we'd eaten our prizes and then we took turns on the tire swing until it was time for lunch. The perogies were delicious and the tiny cakes were iced with different colors—pink, blue, and yellow. Mrs. Knowles gave us one of each color. I ate the pink and yellow cakes but asked if I could save the blue one for my Uncle Roger. Mrs. Knowles wrapped it for me in waxed paper and told me I was a nice girl.

After lunch we threw a stick for Marcy's dog Ruffy to fetch.

"Ruffy is a *very* smart dog!" Marcy told me. "I never even had to train him to fetch—he just knew what to do all on his own."

That didn't seem like a very big deal to me but I didn't say so. Instead, I said, "He's okay, I guess. Not like the dog that I rescued *my* pet from."

"What kind of pet?" Marcy wanted to know.

"A magpie," I told her. "Uncle Roger had to bandage his wing and I'm in charge of taking care of him until he can fly again. We called him Sammy and he's awfully talkative."

Marcy tried not to look impressed, but I could tell she wished she had a more interesting pet than dumb old stick-fetching Ruffy.

"Sammy just seems to know what I'm saying when I talk to him," I went on. "If I ask him does he want bugs or worms, he points his beak at one of the jars to let me know. And when he's a bit better he's going to ride around on my shoulder everywhere I go."

Marcy interrupted then, which was probably a good thing. I guess I'd spent enough time exaggerating Sammy's talents.

"Hey," she said. "Come and see my room! It's the most perfect princess room you ever saw."

Princesses must like pink a lot, because that was the color of everything in that room. Walls and floor, bedspread and curtains—all different shades of pink. And ruffles! There were ruffles everywhere I looked—on the curtains, atop the dresser, around her bed and pillows, and even around the outside of her picture frames.

"Isn't it beautiful?" Marcy said.

"It sure is pink," I said. "And frilly."

"I know," Marcy giggled. "I'm so lucky! I get to sleep here every night."

After the tour of Marcy's room we went outside, found some sticks, and drew squares for hopscotch. We played that for a while. Then we picked some wildflowers for Mrs. Knowles and took a walk down the road and back. Just before it was time for Uncle Roger to pick me up again, Mrs. Knowles brought us cold lemonade and told me I was welcome to come back anytime, and she hoped I was enjoying my visit with my relations.

"How long will you be here?" she asked.

I explained about Daddy's job and the Marvelous pots and pans and told her it probably wouldn't be much longer.

"Well, it *sounds* like it *could* be until the end of the summer," she said with a big, bright smile. "That would be lovely. Marcy hasn't had a playmate nearby in years."

She might have thought it sounded like a good thing, but *I* sure didn't! The idea of being stuck at Grandma's place for the whole rest of the summer was almost more than I could bear. Of course, I didn't say any of that to her. After all, Grandma might not be the nicest grandmother in the world, but she's still kin and all.

Marcy was talking about the things we could do together if I was around all summer, but I wasn't listening. I was imagining Daddy driving up to Grandma's house, jumping out and picking me up like he used to when I was small—twirling me around in the air and laughing—telling me he'd come to take me home.

Maybe if I thought it hard enough, it would happen sooner. Maybe even today. Why, Daddy could be at Grandma's right now, waiting for me to come back!

A sudden feeling of panic swept over me, and I didn't want to be at Marcy's house anymore. I wished Uncle Roger would hurry up and come for me.

It was another long fifteen minutes before his truck turned in the drive and rumbled to a stop. I thanked Marcy and Mrs. Knowles for having me and for the lovely lunch and said I'd had a wonderful time. Mostly it was true, even if Marcy *was* kind of bossy and braggy. It had been fun to have someone to play with instead of going around as quiet as a mouse doing chores.

But now I had the strangest feeling in me, and all

I wanted to do was get back to Grandma's house, in case Daddy was there.

"Have a good day, Ellie?" Uncle Roger asked as I climbed up onto the front seat. I nodded and smiled and hoped he couldn't tell a real smile from a pretend one like Daddy can.

"Much obliged to you," Uncle Roger called to Mrs. Knowles, who was standing on the step with Marcy. She said it had been a pleasure to have me, and then she held her hand up and told him to wait.

After disappearing into the house for a minute, she came back with the blue cake I'd saved for him. I'd been in such a hurry to leave I'd forgotten all about it.

He thanked her again and we drove off toward Grandma's. As soon as we were on our way, I felt a lot calmer.

"Now, about this cake," Uncle Roger said. "Do you recommend it, Ellie?"

"I sure do," I told him.

"You don't suppose it will spoil my supper, do you? I don't want to get a scolding."

"Don't worry," I said, indignant at the thought of Grandma scolding a full-grown man like Uncle Roger. "It won't fill you up. I had two of them and that was after I'd already eaten three whole perogies."

Uncle Roger smiled and nodded at me, then popped the cake into his mouth. That was when I saw his shoulders shaking so I knew he'd only been joking. Still, I wouldn't put it past Grandma.

I tried not to hope too hard as we got close to Grandma's, so when we turned off the road and there was no sign of Daddy's car, I told myself it didn't matter. It had been silly to think he would be back so soon anyway.

As Uncle Roger's truck came to a stop, he reached over and put his hand on my shoulder.

"That was real nice of you," he said, "saving me some cake. Thank you, Ellie."

That made me feel good.

So I can't explain why, suddenly, all I wanted to do was cry.

Eleven

After being away for a day, it was even harder to settle back into the routine at Grandma's house. The worst part of it was that I couldn't seem to do one single thing right. I folded the clothes wrong and Grandma sighed and folded almost everything over. I swept too hard and stirred up dust when I was cleaning the floor. I missed food when I washed dishes and took hold of the silverware wrong when I was drying.

You'd have thought there'd have been at least one thing I could do right, but if there was, I never heard about it. Sometimes I wasn't even sure what the problem was, but I always knew there *was* one by the sound of Grandma's heavy sigh.

Sammy was a big help at those times. Some days I'd go out there and talk and talk to him. You'd swear by the way he tilted his head and looked at me, that he knew just what I was saying. At times it was like he was rescuing me instead of the other way around.

Now and then, Uncle Roger would mention that Marcy would be coming to visit soon. I think he meant to cheer me up but it didn't always work that way. I couldn't help but remember the claims I'd made about Sammy. Marcy was sure to want to see him do the tricks I'd bragged about. She was also sure to think Grandma's house was shabby and gloomy next to hers. And goodness only knew what she might think of Grandma herself.

At first it seemed so far off, but then, before I knew it, Marcy was going to be coming the very next day. I didn't even mind that Grandma gave me extra chores that morning. The less Marcy had to find fault with, the better. After lunch Grandma called out to me to come and help her make pies. I felt my heart sink right into my shoes at those words. I'd never had any part of making a pie before. My feet slowed down but I still got to the kitchen faster than I wanted to.

"Yes, ma'am?" I said. I wished Daddy could see how well I was doing, remembering my manners.

"Wash your hands and go to the table," Grandma said. As soon as I'd done this, she plunked a large bowl down in front of me. Peeking over the rim I saw that it was almost half full of flour. To that, Grandma added a large blob of something pale and shiny. A little puff of flour rose up around it as the blob landed.

"Here," she said, passing me a pair of butter knives. "Blend in the lard."

I looked at the knives and then at the contents of the bowl. Obviously, there was something I didn't know about mixing lard into flour. I picked up the knives, wondering why I couldn't just use a spoon.

Grandma was at the sink, washing rhubarb and trimming the ends off the stalks. Her back was to me. I opened my mouth to ask her what I was supposed to do, but no words came out.

Instead, I reached into the bowl and began to stir the lard with one of the knives. All this did was push the lump up against one side of the bowl. That forced a small burst of flour up, out, and onto the table.

My stomach started to hurt.

At this rate, the flour would soon be all over the table. Clearly, stirring wasn't going to work. Maybe I was supposed to chop the lard up. I stabbed into it and started to cut pieces off. They fell on top of each other. When I tried to stir them around (slowly and gently this time) they stuck together. I could see that the lard wasn't getting any more mixed in with the flour than it had been when I started.

I looked down at the table. The second knife sat there, clean and untouched. I wondered again why Grandma had given me two knives. Maybe I needed to use them both at the same time. After thinking about it for a moment, I stuck the clean knife down into the lard. It must be that I was supposed to hold it in place while I chopped off pieces. As I did this, I stirred the smaller chunks unto the flour. All that did was coat them with flour, but at least they weren't sticking together this time.

This kept me busy for a few minutes, so I hardly noticed Grandma turning to look across the room at me.

"*What* are you *doing*?" she demanded. Her words were sharp and they came at me unexpectedly, which nearly made me knock the bowl over.

My heart pounded at the very thought of what would happen if I'd sent flour flying all over the kitchen. I gulped and swallowed, trying to make myself answer. At last I squeaked out a reply.

"Mixing the lard and flour like you said, Grandma."

Grandma shook her head. She sighed loudly and

dried her hands on her apron. I cringed as she crossed the floor and peered down into the bowl.

"This isn't right," she said. Her words were quick and sharp. "Who taught you how to make pastry?"

"No one," I said.

"What? At your age?" She sounded indignant. Then she saw my face and the message that was on it found its way to her. I saw it happen. I saw her realize that there had been no one to show me things like making pastry.

I saw her remember that I have no mother.

Grandma's face changed. It seemed to fall a little. Then she pressed her mouth together so tight that her lips nearly disappeared. She took a long, slow breath in through her nose and cleared her throat.

"So, I will show you, then."

All of a sudden the table blurred in front of me. I told myself I wasn't going to cry, but I knew it was already too late. A tear slid down my cheek and hit the wooden surface with a gentle *plop*.

Grandma stiffened as she leaned over me. I thought for sure she was going to yell at me for crying like a baby, but she said nothing at all. Instead, she put her hands over mine and showed me how to slice through the lard with both knives at once. Her hands moved mine slowly at first and then got faster as the blades slid toward and past each other again and again.

I swallowed hard and took a deep breath. That helped me stop crying, but the tears that were already built up were still there. I hoped Grandma hadn't noticed that I'd been crying. I thought I could probably wipe the tears away before she saw them.

All the while, Grandma's hands held mine while we slashed away at the lard. I realized with a start that her arms were around me. Not *really*, but sort of, because of the way she was standing behind me and showing me what to do.

It was a strange feeling. I closed my eyes and pretended, just for a minute, that she was hugging me, like any normal grandmother would do.

I pretended that she loved me.

Twelve

I felt like I'd been sitting by the lone window in the parlor for hours, waiting for Marcy to arrive. There wasn't much to see watching the road, either— just a trail of dust billowing up behind a passing car now and then. But finally, one of the cars stopped at the end of the driveway and turned in.

It was Mrs. Knowles all right, and I could see Marcy bouncing up and down beside her.

I slid off the chair and made a beeline for the front door, flinging it open just as Mrs. Knowles and Marcy reached it.

"Hello, Ellie," Mrs. Knowles said. She smiled quickly, the way people do if they're in a hurry. "Is your grandmother here?"

"Yes, ma'am," I said. I turned to go fetch Grandma, but she was already clomping along the hall.

"Mrs. Acklebee," Mrs. Knowles said with another hasty smile. "I'm terribly sorry to have to bother you, but I need to ask a favor."

Grandma's face didn't change but she nodded, like she was giving Marcy's mother permission to go ahead and talk.

"My sister, Dottie—I guess you know she's expecting her first child. Well, her time has come and the midwife has no one there to help. Now, I know you're only expecting Marcy to stay until the middle of the afternoon, but I was wondering—"

"Go," Grandma said at once. "The child can stay here as long as you need her to."

"Oh, thank you *so* much!" Mrs. Knowles said. She leaned down to Marcy and murmured a few instructions about being a good girl and minding what she was told. Then she hugged her daughter, kissed her cheek, and told Grandma she'd be back as soon as she could.

"No hurry," Grandma said. Mrs. Knowles thanked her again and was gone.

Marcy squealed and gave me a huge hug. She jumped up and down a little at the same time, which nearly knocked me over.

I didn't mind.

Grandma frowned but she didn't tell Marcy not to jump or squeal. She didn't even give her a mean look. Instead, she told us to go play until lunchtime.

"I guess you can show me that bird you were telling me about," Marcy said.

I led her out to the shed, hoping Sammy might behave himself today. Of course, that didn't happen. The second I opened the door, he set up the awfullest racket you ever heard. But not just then! He screeched and hollered at us like crazy the whole time we were in there.

I gave him some flies but he'd eaten just a little while earlier, so even the food didn't tempt him into better behavior.

"REE! REE! REE!" he yelled on and on.

"He's pretty rude," Marcy commented. "I thought you said he did other things. It doesn't sound like he does anything except scream!"

"He's not hungry right now," I said. "And he's not used to other people."

"Didn't I hear you brag about how he listens to *you?*"

"He does," I said, "but right now he feels like talking."

"You call that talking? Some birds learn to say real words, you know," she told me. "Mr. Fletcher had a

71

bird that could say 'bad kitty' and 'sunny day.' It used to live at his store."

"What happened to it?" I glanced at Sammy doubtfully. I was pretty sure he was never going to learn to say real words.

"It died."

"Oh. Well, Sammy here hasn't learned to talk…yet," I said. "But he might, if he stays long enough."

Marcy burst out laughing. "That bird of yours," she said when she could speak again, "couldn't talk if it was here for a hundred years."

I felt kind of indignant at that, even though I'd been thinking the very same thing just a moment before Marcy said it.

Sammy never stopped his screeching even after we left the shed and walked across the yard.

"So, what is there to do around here?" Marcy asked.

"You want to hunt for some bugs and worms for Sammy?" I asked.

"No," Marcy answered. She looked cross at the very idea of it. "I want to do something fun. And who cares about a dumb old bird anyway? There are millions of them around here."

I cared, but I didn't say anything back.

"Let's play with your toys," Marcy suggested. "How many dolls do you have?"

"I didn't bring my dolls with me," I said, carefully avoiding admitting I only had one doll. "I have a coloring book of circus pictures, though, and nearly half the pages aren't colored yet."

"Plain old coloring is boring," Marcy said. "We could draw our own pictures and color them and have a contest like we did at my house. That was fun."

"Grandma has no plain paper," I said. I had no idea, really, whether she did or not, but I wasn't going to ask her for any, that was for sure. And there was no way I was going to ask her to judge a contest like Marcy's mom had done. I could picture Grandma telling us that all of our drawings were terrible.

"Well, I only color in boring old books when it's raining or I have a tummy ache and have to stay in bed," Marcy told me.

Tummy aches were of interest to me. I'd had several pains in my stomach in the last few weeks. I thought perhaps Marcy knew of a remedy, but before I could ask her about it, she went on.

"Anyway, I have a coloring book of safari animals. Safari animals are a lot better than circus animals."

"They are?"

"Everyone knows that. Because they're not in cages."

"Oh," I said.

Marcy sighed. "So, do you have anything else to play with?" she asked. She looked bored and a little grumpy.

"I didn't bring my toys with me," I explained. There was a racing feeling inside me, a kind of panic to hurry and think of something. I was afraid Marcy was wishing she wasn't there.

"I know! Let's pretend we're going for a drive," Marcy said, pointing to Uncle Roger's truck. Before I could even get my mouth open, she ran over to it, pulled open the door, and slid into the driver's seat. I followed slowly and got in on the passenger side.

"I don't know if we should be in here," I said.

"Why not? My daddy lets me play in our car anytime I want. And sometimes when we go for a drive, he even lets me sit with him and steer."

"I still don't think we should be in here without asking Uncle Roger first," I said. I felt like I should say more to persuade her, but that was all I could get out. Marcy's talk about her father made me think about driving along with Daddy, and it felt like something was squeezing my chest.

Before I could get rid of the tight feeling so that I could say something more about it, Marcy started jiggling the gear shift and cranking the wheel back and forth.

And then it happened.

The truck started to move.

Thirteen

Now, the truck wasn't moving fast at all—there's not much of a slope in the ground, but it was still pretty scary to feel ourselves moving forward.

Marcy screamed. It was good and loud too, but it wasn't one bit helpful.

"Marcy!" I hollered, trying to make myself heard over her screeches. "Step on the brake!"

I don't know if Marcy didn't hear me or if she was in too much of a panic to take in what I was saying, but she decided to do something else. Instead of trying to stop the truck, she grabbed the door handle and yanked on it until the door started to open.

But then it seemed that she forgot to let go of the handle, because as the door swung outward, she went right along with it. At first, her legs and feet stayed inside the truck. She kind of looked like a hammock made of a little girl, hung between the door and the seat.

Let me tell you, the shrieks that came out of her then were something! I didn't even bother trying to talk to her after that. It seemed the truck was moving a little faster, and as it did, there was less and less of Marcy inside.

And then she lurched forward and disappeared!

I threw myself across the seat to where I could see her. She was screaming even louder than before, and I didn't blame her. The back tire had rolled forward, catching the material from her skirt under it. In a few more inches, that truck was going to run right over Marcy!

There was no time to get turned around. I nose-dived toward the pedals and shoved my hands hard on the one on the right, not knowing which of the three was the brake. Nothing happened. I let go of it and pushed down the middle one and the truck jolted to a stop.

Marcy was still wailing her head off when Grandma showed up.

"Oh, oh, oh," Grandma said.

"Help me!" Marcy sobbed. "Don't let the truck run over me!"

"Stop that and listen!" Grandma said sharply. "I'll see if I can pull your skirt loose; you try to wriggle out."

The next few moments were filled with the sounds of grunts and groans. I could tell when Grandma got the skirt free because she fell backward and landed on the ground with a thud. Right after that, Marcy stood up, still crying while she brushed herself off.

Grandma reached out and steadied Marcy, then she peered into the truck at me.

"Come out of there now, Elizabeth," she said sternly.

"I can't, Grandma."

"Why not?"

"If I let go of the brake, the truck will start moving again," I said. "It will hit the barn."

Grandma glanced toward the barn and then stared at the pedal I was holding down. "This pedal is the brake?" she asked. "You're sure?"

"I'm sure," I said. It had to be—it had stopped the truck from killing Marcy, who chose that moment to speak up.

"I *told* Ellie not to touch anything!" Marcy said. "I told her we shouldn't be in that truck at all. She wouldn't listen, and look what happened! Why, she nearly got me *killed* is what!"

I felt my mouth fall right open in shock at what that lying Marcy Knowles was saying. But before I could protest, Grandma was speaking again.

"Roger will have to come," she said. "He'll know what to do. Marcy, you run through to the third field from here and find him. He's on the tractor so you'll see him, no trouble. Tell him to come home at once. Quickly now!"

Marcy hesitated, but she did what Grandma told her. As soon as she was gone I took a deep breath and said, "Grandma, I didn't—"

But Grandma held her hand up to stop me. "I know what the truth is," she said. After a pause she added, "And something else I know is who screamed and who used her head to do something smart."

I couldn't quite believe my ears. A huge feeling of happiness swelled up inside me. The feeling stayed there while I waited, even though my arms were starting to shake from the strain of holding down that pedal.

Before long, the shaking had become pain and it was all I could do to keep from letting go. It seemed to take an awful long time for Uncle Roger to get there. I heard him first, his feet pounding along the ground.

Grandma's head turned in the direction of the sound just as he called out, "Ellie! Is she all right, Ma?"

"She's fine," Grandma told him. "No need to make a fuss."

Uncle Roger was out of breath when he reached the driver's side of the truck. He reached in and pulled on something. "There," he panted. "The hand brake will hold 'er now, Ellie. You can come on out."

It was a huge relief to finally be able to let go of the pedal. When I scrambled out of the truck, my arms started to rise up in the air all on their own. I'd hardly reached the ground when I felt myself being swung up and pulled tight against Uncle Roger's chest.

"I'm not cross at you," he said. "Not at all. But I don't want you to play in the truck anymore."

I knew right then that Marcy had told him the same lie she'd told Grandma. I waited for Grandma to tell him the truth. But she just turned around and went back into the house without another word. And then it was too late for me to say anything, because Marcy was coming through the field, gasping and sweaty, her face as red as a ripe tomato.

Uncle Roger let me down and slid into the truck. He pressed his foot on the pedal on the left and pushed on the gear shift with his hand. That reminded me of how Marcy had bumped the gear shift just before the truck started to move.

When he got back out, I said, nice and loud, "Marcy, my uncle fixed the thing you were jiggling and he doesn't want us to get in the truck again."

"Who'd want to get in there again anyway?" Marcy said.

"Well, like I said a while ago—" I began, but Marcy cut me off by grabbing my hand and yanking me away from there.

"I hope you didn't tell on me," she muttered as soon as we were a ways off from Uncle Roger.

"Why shouldn't I tell on you?" I asked crossly.

"Because I'm the guest and that's the rule."

"What kind of dumb rule is that?"

"It's just the rule. And anyway, if you did something wrong at my house, I would take the blame for it for you."

I doubted that, but I didn't say anything else to Marcy. She might be bossy and she might tell lies, but she was the only friend I had here. I didn't want to go through the whole summer with no one to play with.

With Marcy, it seemed as soon as she said something, it was settled, whether anyone else might agree or not.

"I know what we can do now!" she said, just as if the whole truck thing had never happened. "Let's go ask your grandmother if we can make cookies."

Fourteen

Grandma wasn't in the kitchen. That was lucky because Marcy just tromped right in. I had to call her back to the doorway.

"We have to take our shoes off," I whispered. I'd forgotten the shoe rule a few times when I first got there, and Grandma had asked me, did I think I was in the barn? I wanted Grandma to see that I wasn't letting Marcy treat her kitchen like a barn either.

Marcy stepped on the heels of her shoes to get them off, then sent them skittering up against the wall. I was straightening them out when I heard Grandma's heavy step coming down the hall. She stopped just inside the kitchen door and looked back and forth at Marcy and me.

Marcy stood there staring at me and waiting. I knew she was expecting me to go ahead and ask about the cookies, but the look on Grandma's face stopped me. I opened my mouth to speak a few times, but nothing came out. I probably looked good and silly—like Sheila's goldfish, who spends his days opening and closing his mouth for no good reason as far as I know.

"Ellie wants to know if we can make some cookies."

I don't know who was more surprised—me or Grandma. We both turned to Marcy at the same time.

"What?" Grandma said. I kept right on imitating Sheila's goldfish.

"Cookies. Me 'n Ellie were wondering if we could make some."

Grandma frowned.

"Oh, sorry!" Marcy said quickly. "I meant *Ellie and I*. Momma tells me about that all the time, but I still forget."

"What kind of cookies?" Grandma said.

Marcy glanced at me. If she was looking for a suggestion, she didn't get one. "I like oatmeal raisin," she said. "They're my favorite."

Grandma frowned again. "Roger doesn't like raisins," she said. "We will make sugar cookies."

"Okay," Marcy said. She clapped her hands.

"Mmmm! Sugar cookies are yummy, too. Don't you just love them, Ellie?

"Don't you, Ellie? Don't you?" Marcy repeated before I could even answer. She skipped around the room. I saw Grandma's forehead crease, but I couldn't think of a way to tell Marcy she shouldn't be skipping in the kitchen. I couldn't remember the reason for it.

· "Yes," I said finally. "Sugar cookies are good."

I hoped I hadn't jinxed it. Sheila says that you have to be careful when something good is going to happen. She says that if you're too happy about it, that might keep it from happening at all. Daddy says that's silly superstition, but I don't like to take any chances, just in case.

But everything was okay. We helped beat the shortening and sugar, and then we added the eggs while Grandma mixed up the dry ingredients and measured the milk. Once the cookie dough was ready, Marcy rolled it into balls and I pressed the balls down on the cookie sheets with a glass that had been dipped in sugar.

The recipe made sixty-three cookies, and you wouldn't believe how good the kitchen smelled when they were baking. That was nothing compared to the taste, though. We all had one when they were still warm from the oven—even Grandma. Those cookies were big and soft and so delicious that Marcy and I agreed later on we could have eaten a whole dozen between us.

When we'd finished washing the dishes and cleaning up from making the cookies, it was time for lunch. Marcy and I set the table while Grandma fried up some leftover potatoes and wieners with chopped onions. Just before she served it, she cracked some eggs over top of the whole thing, added a good dose of paprika and covered it for a few minutes. Then she lifted portions out with a big spatula and everything was stuck together with the eggs.

My mouth was watering by the time Uncle Roger came along, bringing the scent of the fields with him. He washed his hands at the sink and sat down at the table.

"Something sure smells good in here," he said right after he'd said grace. "Is it you two girls?"

"No!" Marcy squealed. "We made cookies!"

Uncle Roger looked over at the counter where the cooling racks were sitting. His eyes got big and round like he couldn't quite believe what he was seeing. That made us laugh since he'd been right there beside them, washing his hands a minute ago.

"Cookies!" he said, pretending to be surprised. "Well, well, well. What do you know!"

Like most grown-ups, Uncle Roger wasn't very good at make-believe.

"The food is getting cold," Grandma said. So we all quieted down and ate our lunch. Even Marcy stopped chattering after a couple of stern looks from Grandma. All you could hear after that was the kitchen clock and the sounds of our forks scraping along the plates.

The food was real good, even though it was leftovers. I didn't like to admit it, but it tasted better than when Daddy makes potatoes and wieners.

But at least when Daddy and I eat, we talk to each other instead of just listening to the sounds our forks make.

Fifteen

U ncle Roger saved the day after lunch. I'd been wondering what we could do that Marcy *wouldn't* complain about, and I was trying to think of something fun when he spoke up.

"I don't suppose you girls would be interested in being any taller."

"Being *taller?*" Marcy and I echoed.

"Sure. All you need are some magic sticks."

"Magic!" Marcy clapped her hands.

"Roger…?" It seemed that Grandma was going to ask something and then stopped. Whatever it was, Uncle Roger seemed to understand.

"It's all right, Ma," he told her. "I made these before lunch. They're brand new.

"Come on," he told us then. "I'll just show you

girls what to do, and then you can come back and help clean up from lunch."

"No, no," Grandma said, shooing us away like we were flies. "Guests don't help with the chores. You girls go and play."

Marcy and I were out the door with Uncle Roger in a flash. He led us to the side of the barn where we could see four slender poles leaning against the tired gray wood.

"Stilts!" Marcy cried as soon as she saw them. "I love stilts! I'm very, very good at walking on them. Momma says it's because I'm naturally graceful."

"Izzat right?" Uncle Roger said. He picked up the stilts and carried them back across the yard. We followed along like baby ducks after their mother.

When we reached the clothesline stand, Uncle Roger stopped and motioned for us to go up the steps to the platform.

"Stop when you get about level with these here wedges," he told us. He pointed to triangle-shaped pieces of wood that were nailed to the poles.

We did as we were told and Marcy, who insisted on going first because of all her experience, took hold of the poles, stepped onto the wedges, and took a few steps. Then her arms started to wobble, the poles jerked about wildly, and she came crashing down.

"Are you sure these are made right?" she asked crossly as she picked herself up and brushed away some dirt and grass that was clinging to her.

"They're stilts," Uncle Roger said. "What could be wrong with them?"

Marcy's eyebrows ploughed together in a frown but she got over her anger fast. "Anyway, it's ages and ages since I was on stilts," she said. "I probably just need to practice. Then you won't be able to *believe* how good I am on them."

"No, we probably won't," Uncle Roger agreed. I saw a smile try to bust out on his face, but he fought it off. Then he showed me how to get on the stilts, and he guided me while I took my first few steps.

I was pretty shaky at it and I figured I'd soon be landing on my behind, too. But Uncle Roger told us that if we felt we were losing control, we should lean forward a bit and jump down.

Marcy made another attempt. She did all right for a few steps before she lost her balance and landed on the ground again.

"I did that on purpose," she claimed. "I just realized how thirsty I am, so I got down to get a drink of water."

"Well, now. I'd best be getting back to work," Uncle Roger said, but he didn't move.

"Uncle Roger?" I said. "Did you and my mother have stilts?"

"We sure did," he said. "We used to race on 'em and make bets to see who could stay up the longest. Your mom won most of the time and I'd end up doing one of her chores. That's usually what we bet— a chore."

I tried to picture my mother as a little girl and Uncle Roger as a little boy, playing together right in this yard. I wondered if their stilts were like the ones Uncle Roger had just made. And then I remembered my grandmother's face when she'd said Uncle Roger's name in that strange tone of voice earlier, and I knew she'd thought that he was going to let me use my mother's stilts. Mostly, I knew she didn't want me touching them.

"Do you still have those stilts?" I asked.

"They're here," he said, "up in the rafters. But the wood is old and dry and starting to split. They wouldn't be safe anymore."

"Did you make these new ones just for me and Marcy?" I asked.

He nodded. "There was nothing to it," he said.

"But I never used stilts before, and now Marcy

and I have something to do," I said. "Thank you, Uncle Roger."

"Aw," he said, like he was brushing away my thanks. But his face looked pleased, and watching it, I discovered something odd. Uncle Roger's burn wasn't nearly as noticeable as it was when I first met him.

I went into the kitchen and was surprised to see Marcy standing beside Grandma, drying dishes and talking.

"*I* felt like helping," Marcy said with her chin up in the air. "I don't think your grandmother should have to do all the work by herself, Ellie."

"Elizabeth helps me every day," Grandma said.

"My mother says I'm the best helper there ever was," Marcy claimed.

"That's nice," Grandma said. "Elizabeth, would you sweep the floor, please? You always do an excellent job of it."

I picked up the broom and began to sweep the floor extra carefully.

"I can't believe I fell off the stilts today," Marcy said. "Mother says I have natural grace and balance, and I could be in the ballet if I had lessons. And Daddy told me one time that I was the best stilt-walker he ever saw."

Grandma didn't give Marcy much encouragement—a grunt now and then—but that didn't stop Marcy from bragging on and on. It was a relief when the chores were all finished and it was time to go back outside. Marcy was out the door like a bolt, but I held back for a minute or two.

"Is there anything else you'd like me to do before I go play, Grandma?" I asked.

"No. You go on with your friend." It seemed her voice was just a little softer than usual. It gave me a flash of courage.

"All right," I said. "And thank you…for letting me and Marcy make cookies."

Grandma's chin lifted and her eyes seemed to settle on the tired old wallpaper over the stove. "Roger likes sugar cookies," she said.

"Yes, ma'am," I said, but as I turned to walk away, Grandma spoke again.

"But you're welcome, Elizabeth."

Marcy was already on the clothesline stand, holding onto one pair of stilts. She shouted, "I'm over here, Ellie!" as if I might not notice her there.

I got there quick enough and we both balanced ourselves on the stilts and took a few wobbly steps before we lost control. Remembering my Uncle Roger's instructions, we pitched forward and then jumped down.

Laughing, we raced back to the stand and tried again. And again. We lurched and veered off course. Down we went over and over. If it wasn't for Uncle Roger's help in telling us how to keep from crashing, we'd have been bruised from head to toe. I'm sure if anyone was watching they'd have thought we were the most hopeless stilt-walkers in the entire world. Maybe we were, but it sure was fun.

Even so, it wasn't long before we were managing more than just a few steps. By the end of the afternoon, we could both walk around for a few minutes at a time.

"My uncle said he and my mom used to race," I told Marcy when we were taking a break and lying back on a shaded patch of grass.

"Race?" Marcy looked doubtful. "You want to try it?"

"Nah. They had a lot more practice than us," I said.

"Oh, well, maybe some other time," Marcy said. She sounded disappointed, but her face looked relieved.

We were just starting to get tired of playing on the stilts when Mrs. Knowles arrived to pick Marcy up.

"It's a girl!" she called as soon as she was out of the car. "Marcy, honey, you have a new cousin!"

Marcy didn't seem very excited at her mother's news. She said something about crying babies, but her voice was too low and mumbled for me to hear it clearly.

"And you'll be happy to know that Aunt Dottie is doing just fine," Mrs. Knowles added.

"Hello!" came Grandma's voice. She was just coming out the front door. "Did I hear you say the little one has arrived?"

"Yes, a girl."

"The baby is healthy—everything went well?"

"Yes, thank you," Mrs. Knowles said. "Dottie is tired, of course, but she and the baby are both fine."

"Good, good," Grandma said, smiling. Her face crinkled and her dark eyes almost disappeared in the folds.

"I hope Marcy behaved herself for you," Mrs. Knowles went on.

"Oh, yes," said Grandma.

"We made cookies and played on stilts," Marcy announced.

"You did! Well, isn't that nice." Mrs. Knowles smiled at Grandma like it had all been her idea. "I can't thank you enough for watching her for me."

"It was no problem," Grandma said. "But wait here one moment. I have something for the little one."

She disappeared inside and reappeared with a beautiful new baby quilt.

"What lovely stitch work!" Mrs. Knowles said. "I know Dottie will be thrilled."

"Did you make it?" Marcy asked. When Grandma nodded, she said, "You must have worked on it all day!"

And then, you wouldn't believe it, but Grandma laughed. Mrs. Knowles did too, and she explained to Marcy that quilts—even small ones—take a long time to make. When they were gone, I gathered my nerve up and asked Grandma when she had made it.

"I start one whenever I hear news that there will be a new baby," she said. "I like to keep busy."

She glanced down at me. "It would be good for you to learn this too. Life is about work, not play."

Sixteen

After Marcy's visit, the next few days were pretty dismal. Grandma seemed extra grumpy and hardly spoke to me, except to give me chores to do or remind me to be quiet.

One afternoon I was sweeping off the back step when she came along.

"You *like* to disobey, is that it?" she asked.

"No, ma'am." I knew I didn't have to ask what I'd done wrong. If there was one thing that seemed to make her happy, it was explaining my shortcomings.

"So, why do you make this noise?"

It took me a few seconds to figure out what noise she meant. Then I realized that I'd been singing. I told her I was sorry and I'd try harder.

"Heedless girl," she muttered as she walked away.

I finished sweeping in silence, reminding myself that it was only for a little while longer and that Daddy would soon have sold enough Marvelous pots and pans to come get me. I missed him all the time, but I missed him the most when Grandma made me feel bad.

Usually, when I got to feeling real lonesome for my daddy I could fight off tears by breathing in huge gulps of air and holding them, but not this time.

They spilled out of my eyes and fell onto the steps, forming splotches of wet on the sun-bleached wood even as I swept. Somehow, I knew if Grandma saw me crying this time, it would make things worse. I stood the broom up against the door frame and ran across the yard with only one thought in my head—escaping her watchful eyes and ears.

I'd meant to go out behind the barn, but as I got close to it I could see that the side door was open just a little. A shuffling kind of sound inside told me that Uncle Roger was in there, and without thinking, I stuck my head in and peered around.

It was hard to see at first. There were only a few small windows in there, though a bit more light did get in through all the spaces between the wall's boards. It was hard to say if the light helped or not because it mostly seemed to show up the dusty haziness in the air.

Uncle Roger was sitting on an overturned pail, holding a long piece of wood that was curved on both ends. He looked over almost at once, probably because the door squeaked a bit when my head nudged it.

"Hello, Ellie's head," he called out.

I swallowed and blinked and cleared my throat a little, then answered him hello back.

"Come on in, and bring the rest of Ellie with you," he said.

I knew there were streaks down my face from the tears but it didn't seem likely Uncle Roger would be able to see them in the dark of the barn. I swiped at my cheeks to brush the wet away and then stepped in and walked toward him, stopping about ten feet away.

"There's a milking stool over there," he said, gesturing with his thumb. "Bring it here and have a sit-down."

I got the stool and brought it over. It was short, like it had been made for someone like me who didn't have very long legs.

"This here," he said, nodding at the curved piece of wood he was holding, "is a handmade swingle tree. It goes on the horse's traces when we're setting up to haul big loads."

I looked it over carefully and nodded like he'd just confirmed what I'd been thinking. Actually, I'd never even heard of a swingle tree before and couldn't begin to picture how it worked.

Whatever he'd been doing, it seemed he was just finishing when I got there, because he stood up, crossed the barn, and hung it on a hook beside some other odd things. They looked like tools of some sort, though nothing I'd ever seen before.

I stood when he did. "I'd better get back to my chores now," I said as he started back toward me. But my feet didn't move.

"Aw, come on outside and set a spell," Uncle Roger said. "See what the sky has to say."

"Skies can't talk," I said, but I went with him and sat down against a bank of hay on the far side of the barn. When he leaned back and stared up at the sky, I did too.

"What do you think this here sky's telling us?" he asked.

"I don't know," I said, watching the clusters of small clouds. "Looks like it might be gathering for a rainstorm."

"Could be." He didn't sound convinced. After a bit, he said, "Your ma would have called this a tumbleweed sky."

"How come?"

"She said these kinds of clouds were dry and

dusty and blowing along like a bunch of tumble-weeds. One time she told me they were like people who'd forgotten how to love—looking normal on the outside, but withered up and empty on the inside." He shook his head and smiled sadly. "Maggie saw things different, that's for sure."

I didn't know what to say to that, so I just stayed quiet and hoped he'd keep on talking. But when he spoke again, it was just to ask me how I was getting along with Grandma.

"Fine," I lied.

He looked at me for a long minute, like he was figuring something out, but all he said was, "Those cookies you made the other day—did you know they were your ma's favorite kind?"

"Grandma said they were *your* favorite," I said.

Uncle Roger shook his head. "Nope. I like the ones with dates in the middle."

"Do you think Grandma forgot?" I asked.

"Can't see it," he said. He put his arms up and folded them behind his head. "No sir, my guess would be that your grandma wanted to make those cookies for you."

"For *me*?" I couldn't have been more surprised if he'd told me the hay we were lying on was going to be spun into gold.

"Sure. But I don't suppose she could admit it. So she had to let on they were for me."

I thought about that for a bit. Uncle Roger just stayed quiet and let me. I think that might be what I like the most about Uncle Roger—he doesn't try to persuade you about things like most grown-ups.

"I think they were the best cookies I ever tasted," I said after a few minutes.

"Maybe they'll be your favorite, too," Uncle Roger commented. "Just like your ma. Maybe people inherit taste in cookies the same way they inherit eye color and such."

"Do you really think so?"

"I don't see why not." He sat forward and pulled up his knees, circling them with his arms. I did the same and we stayed that way for a few quiet minutes. Then Uncle Roger told me he really should be getting back to work.

"But you know where I am most of the time," he said. "One of the fields, usually. So you come find me anytime you feel like having a visit."

I felt lighter and happier as I headed back to the house and Grandma's stern face. I even tried not to let it bother me too much when Grandma asked me if I'd been hiding, trying to get out of helping with the chores and did I think she was there to wait on me?

I talked to Sammy about it all later—how mean Grandma was and how hard it was to be there.

"Some days I just feel like a prisoner, trapped in this horrible old house," I told him. "I know Grandma is feeding me and giving me a place to live while Daddy gets back on his feet, but I just can't find it in my heart to feel thankful. It's hard to be grateful when you're sad and lonely and just want to be back in your own home."

Sammy tilted his head sideways like he was truly trying to sympathize, but I was probably imagining that.

That night at bedtime, I prayed a prayer that Daddy would be the best Marvelous pots and pans salesman ever so he could come back for me soon.

I don't guess that's the kind of prayer God really wants to hear. Daddy says we should always ask Him to do His will, but I didn't want to take a chance in case His will wasn't the same as what I wanted. Not if it meant I had to stay with Grandma Acklebee one minute longer than I absolutely had to.

Seventeen

"I 'll have to go into town tomorrow morning," Uncle Roger said the next day when we were all at the table having headcheese sandwiches and tomato soup for lunch.

Grandma looked up at him questioningly. I guess trips to town in the middle of the week aren't that usual.

"Broken part on the tractor," he said. "I thought Ellie could come along with me. And we can stop in at the Knowles's place so she and Marcy can make plans for another visit."

Grandma opened her mouth and it wasn't hard to figure out what she might say to that. But she saw the look on Uncle Roger's face and it seemed to be saying there wasn't going to be any arguing about it. Her mouth hung open for a bit and you could tell she was struggling, the way it was quivering.

In the end, she forced it closed and went back to her soup. Her hand trembled as she lifted each spoonful and I could see her jaw muscles working.

It was so peculiar. For the first time since I'd been there, I started to wonder why Grandma gave in to Uncle Roger all the time. Anyone could see she didn't *want* to, and yet she did.

Whatever the reason, I was only too glad to be going to town again the next day. I made up my mind that when it got to be bedtime, I would watch out my window carefully for the first star.

Marcy wasn't such a great friend—not like Judy or Sheila at home, but it would still be nice to have something different to do for a day. Maybe even a whole night too—if she asked me to sleep over like she'd said she would the first time I was there.

Only, that made me a bit nervous. What if Grandma said no and even Uncle Roger couldn't persuade her? How would I explain that to Marcy? She sure wasn't the type to keep things to herself. It would be all over the countryside that my own grandmother wouldn't let me sleep at the Knowles' house.

Then I remembered that Daddy would have called that "borrowing worries." He says folks who do that must really *like* to fret, or they'd at least wait and see if there was an actual reason to worry. He says our Heavenly Father doesn't like us going ahead and getting all stirred up about something that hasn't even happened yet and might well never happen at all. He says we ought to just push those thoughts right out of our heads.

I did my best to push the thought out like Daddy says, but I might just as well admit I couldn't completely get rid of it. An uneasy feeling sat on me, and every time I glanced at Grandma's stern face, it was a little worse.

If there's one good thing about fretting ahead of time, it's that it makes you forget about other unpleasant things. Before I knew it, my afternoon chores were done, and I was laying the table for supper and listening for the sound of Uncle Roger's boots thudding down on the step to knock the dirt off before he came into the kitchen.

When he did, he was smiling and holding an envelope, which clean took my mind off everything else.

"Look what I found out in the mailbox," he said, passing it to me. "A letter for Miss Elizabeth Stewart."

Sure enough, my name was right there on the front—in my daddy's handwriting! Maybe there'd be news about when he was coming back for me! I took the letter and ran upstairs to my room. I closed the door tight and sat on the bed to open it. My heart was pounding with joy and excitement.

Dear Ellie, Daddy's letter started. *How are you doing, kiddo?*

I had to swallow all of a sudden, only it was hard to because it felt like something was squeezing my throat from the inside. I took a couple of slow breaths to calm myself down and gave my eyes a quick wipe 'cause they were getting blurry.

I sure miss my girl, I can tell you that much. I don't know how men do it, them that have jobs that call for traveling all the time. Seems like a hollow way of living, spending your days with strangers and your nights in strange beds.

But what am I doing, complaining about me? I could stand about anything, and that's the truth, if I knew you were happy. Only, I know it's hard on you too, being away from your own home and friends and such.

I wish I could tell you things were going great with the pots and pans, but the fact is, sales have been awful slow. Only two sets in the whole time I've been on the road!

Seems not too many folks are wanting cookware at the moment, not even cookware this fine. Why, the other day in Togo, a lady not only turned down my pots and pans, she tried to make me take back a vacuum cleaner she'd bought a while back. She kept insisting she'd bought it from me, and no amount of talk on my part could convince her that it must have been some other salesman. I finally had no choice but to hightail it out of there when she went to fetch the vacuum. As I was driving away, I could see her on her doorstep, shaking her fist.

I called head office yesterday, to tell them I was quitting, only I got talked into giving it one more shot. They gave me a new territory, though I can't imagine why they'd want to hang onto a salesman who can't seem to sell. Charlie, the guy I talked to, promised me a better area and said if I'd stick it out for another couple of weeks they'd increase my commission by five percent.

Last week I was near enough to Moose Jaw to drop by the mill to see what's what. The foreman, Jasper Peterson (you met him at the company picnic last summer) promised me I'd be back on shift by the first week of September at the latest, and his word has always been good.

If things pick up with the pots and pans, I'll keep at this until the end of August. If not, you'll see your old

*man come rolling in about a week and a half after you
get this letter. Either way, be good for your grandmother
and Uncle Roger, and remember to say your prayers
every night.*

    Love,

    Dad

I read the letter four times and then folded it up
and tucked it back into the envelope. Halfway
through the second time I'd given up on not crying.
Now I wished Uncle Roger hadn't given me the letter
until bedtime. Then I wouldn't have to go back
downstairs and face anybody tonight. But maybe
they wouldn't be able to tell how I felt. Just because
Daddy always knows if something is wrong as soon as
he lays eyes on me, that didn't mean they would
too—did it?

I wished I could sneak out to the pump room and
splash water on my eyes before facing them, but that
was about impossible since I'd have to go through the
kitchen to get there. The best I could do was lift my
shirt and wipe the tear marks off my cheeks, dry my
eyes, and take a few good, deep breaths.

It struck me on my way back to the kitchen that
I'd been praying for the wrong thing all this time.
Daddy wasn't going to quit the Marvelous Company

and come back for me sooner if he was selling lots of pots and pans like I'd figured. He only planned to stop if sales were bad.

My mind was occupied with this thought when I reached Grandma's side and sat down at the table. Next to her plate was a second letter from Daddy so I guessed he'd written to tell her the bad news, too.

I snuck a peek at her, expecting to see a big frown on her face, but she just looked normal. Maybe she hadn't read her letter yet and didn't know that she might be stuck with me all the way until the end of August.

Eighteen

I'd just finished feeding Sammy the next day when Uncle Roger popped into the shed.

"I've come to make good on my promise to take you to town," he said. "Say, Sammy's looking a lot better! You must be taking great care of him."

Sammy bobbed his head up and down as if he was agreeing, which made us both laugh. I was proud of how much he'd improved. He hopped around a lot, with his dark little eyes alert and snapping, and he only screeched when he was hungry.

We said goodbye to Sammy and then got into the truck and headed for town. Uncle Roger whistled while he was driving but I didn't know the song—if it was one. I watched out the window. It was nice sitting up front where a person could see pretty much everything around, even if there wasn't much variety in the scenery. Farms and fields—that was about it.

"You like ice cream?" Uncle Roger asked when he'd made his way through the tune.

"Sure," I said. Daddy always bought a brick when it was my birthday, and once in a while for no special reason if he got overtime at the mill. Just thinking about it made my mouth water.

"You should ask your grandmother to make some," Uncle Roger said.

That was the last thing I'd been expecting to hear. I did my best to hide my disappointment, which wasn't easy. There I'd been, thinking I was going to be treated to a cold, delicious ice-cream cone in town, and instead all I was getting was this terrible advice. Ask my grandmother to make ice cream! Brother.

My thoughts must have gotten through onto my face because Uncle Roger said, "Really, you should ask her. Your mother used to pester her for it all the time, and your grandma always said it was a waste of time but she usually ended up making it just the same."

"Oh," I said. I couldn't think of an answer that didn't sound impudent or doubtful. Grandma might have made ice cream for my mother but there was no way she would do it for me.

"You're not convinced," Uncle Roger said. He was smiling.

"She doesn't exactly like me," I said at last. "In case you haven't noticed."

"She doesn't *want* to like you," he said easily, like that was the most normal thing in the world to tell a kid about her grandmother. "But you could win her over, if you wanted to. It just might take a little time."

"Well …," I said, feeling quite put out. "I don't see why I should have to win over my own grandmother."

"You're right; that's not fair," he agreed. Then he fell silent for a bit. When he spoke again, it was to talk about something else.

"That would have been my farm if the barn hadn't burned down."

I looked to my right where he was pointing but there was nothing much to see really. No barn—well, that made sense—but there was no house either, or any other buildings. Just a pile of rocks sitting back a ways from the road. I wondered why they were there.

"Those, rocks, well, that's where the house would have been," he said, as if he'd read my thoughts. "I put the barn up first, got some cattle, and started working the land. The house would have come later on that summer."

"Why didn't you start over?" I asked. "You saved the animals, right?"

"Yes, they were all okay."

"So, why didn't you just build the barn again? And then the house and all?"

Uncle Roger pulled the truck over to the side of the road and turned off the car. He stared at the land for a few minutes before he answered. When he finally spoke, his voice was quiet.

"Didn't seem like there was much reason, after the fire." He touched his face, running his fingers over the scar, though I don't think he realized he was doing it.

"You see, Ellie," he went on, "I was to supposed get married that fall, to a girl named Ellen. Only, after the fire, things changed. I could see she didn't feel the same anymore, what with my face like this. She tried—she really tried—but it was all she could do not to look away every time she saw me."

"What happened?" I asked. I'd never met this Ellen person, but I disliked her anyway.

"I let her go," he said. "Told her it was plain I couldn't make her happy and I didn't mean to marry her if that was the case. She cried about it but I could see she was relieved."

"Do you think you'll ever get back together?"

"Well, now, I don't think it's too likely," Uncle Roger said with a half smile. "She married someone else a few years later."

"I bet he's not as good as you," I said.

"I appreciate your saying so." He chuckled. "But you'd lose that bet. Albert's a fine fellow."

I sat silent, feeling sorry about what had happened to Uncle Roger, but not having any words for it.

"Anyway, a single man has no need of his own farm," he said after a bit. Then he put the truck back into gear and started driving again.

"Maybe you'll marry someone else, someday," I said.

"Maybe," he said, but there was no belief of it in his voice.

"I need to stop off at Cal Dysert's farm for a bit," Uncle Roger said when we were nearly to town. "No need for you to be bored, waiting for me. How about I drop you over at Marcy's place first and you two can get your next visit all figured out while I'm talking to Cal?"

"Okay."

We pulled into the Knowles's driveway a few minutes later and Uncle Roger went to the door with me.

"Be all right for Ellie to stop off here for a bit?" he asked Marcy's mom when she came to answer.

"Cal Dysert asked me to give him a hand with his tractor—shouldn't take more than half an hour or so—and then me 'n Ellie are heading into town."

"Of course," Mrs. Knowles said at once. "Ellie is welcome here anytime at all. Come on in, Ellie."

Uncle Roger tipped his hat. "Much obliged," he said.

Just then I heard my name being yelled, and when I stepped inside I saw Marcy barreling down the stairs toward me.

"I didn't know you were—," she called out as her feet pounded down the steps. Her voice broke off when she slipped on one of the steps near the bottom and came bumping down the last few on her behind— bump, bump, bump. She landed sitting up on the floor at the bottom. Her face was all surprised and cross looking.

I couldn't help laughing but Marcy didn't find it one bit funny.

"What are *you* laughing at, Ellie?" she yelled as her mother helped her to her feet.

"There there, now, Marcy," Mrs. Knowles said. "I don't think there's any harm done."

"Well, how would *you* like it if *you* hurt yourself and *your* friend laughed about it?" Marcy asked her mother.

"I'm sure Ellie doesn't think it's funny that you hurt yourself," Mrs. Knowles said soothingly.

"Well, are you sorry then, Ellie?" Marcy demanded.

"I wasn't laughing about you getting hurt," I said. "I was laughing about the sound you made bumping down the stairs, and the surprised look on your face."

"There, see? Everything is fine," Mrs. Knowles said. She looked back and forth from me to Marcy with a strange smile on her face.

Marcy shrugged. "Let's go to my room," she said, wrestling herself free from her mother's hug.

We tromped up the stairs and into her pink room. Even though I'd seen it before, it still managed to startle me.

"Let's play house," Marcy said as soon as we were inside the door. She went right to her ruffle-edged shelf and began to look the dolls over.

"I can't," I said. I might have sounded glad, but I couldn't help it. I already knew that playing house with Marcy was no fun.

"Why can't you?" she asked.

"Because I'm only here for a short time. Uncle Roger has to help someone with a tractor and then he's coming back to take me to town with him."

Marcy's eyes narrowed. "Why do you have to go to town with him?" she asked. "Just tell him you want to stay here and play with me instead."

"I *want* to go to town with Uncle Roger," I said quickly. "But we can figure out a different day for me to come over if you want."

"Why would I want you to come over a different day if you don't even want to play here today?" Marcy demanded. She plopped down on her bed, crossed her arms and looked away from me.

I stood there silently, wishing I was in Uncle Roger's truck, waiting while he helped Mr. Dysert with the tractor.

"So?" Marcy said. "Are you going to stay today or not?"

"My Uncle Roger wants me to go to town with him," I said. I felt panicky that Marcy was somehow going to make me stay there.

"Who'd want to go to town with him, anyway?" she snapped. "I sure wouldn't go anywhere with someone with an ugly face like that. He looks like a big old lizard monster!"

Her words shocked me so much I almost couldn't speak, and when I did, all I could manage to say was, "Take that back!"

"Why should I?" she said. "It's true. Your whole family is strange and creepy. And your grandmother is so mean that her very own daughter ran away from home and never came back. My mother said it probably did something to her head."

"That's a lie! There's *nothing* wrong with my uncle or my grandmother!" I yelled. "You're a horrible, hateful, bossy person," I went on, "and I wouldn't play with you again if I had to stay here for the rest of my life."

Marcy's mouth fell open but she snapped it closed quick enough and jumped to her feet. "You just get out of my house!" she shrieked. Her eyes were blazing. "Get out this very minute."

I was down the stairs and out the door in a flash, but then I wasn't sure what to do. It didn't seem like I should sit on the porch and wait for Uncle Roger, so I walked down the dusty drive to the edge of the road, and stood there beside the mailbox until my uncle's truck came along to get me.

Nineteen

Uncle Roger looked pretty surprised to find me on the side of the road when he came back for me.

"Anything wrong?" he asked as I climbed up onto the seat.

"I'm never going there again!"

"I see." Uncle Roger was silent for a few moments. Then he said, "Friends squabble now and then. They usually work it out, though."

"She's *not* my friend," I said. "I *hate* her!"

I felt Uncle Roger's eyes looking at me, but I didn't look back.

"Anything you want to tell me about?" he asked.

"No." That came out sounding cross and I felt bad about it, but I really couldn't tell Uncle Roger the horrid things Marcy had said.

He didn't seem to mind, though. Instead, he changed the subject as he pulled the truck back onto the road.

"I've been thinking some about Sammy," he said.

I smiled at the mention of that silly old magpie. "What about him?" I asked.

"Like I said earlier, you've done a great job with him. He's looking pretty good."

Something in his tone told me I might not like what was coming next. "He's a *little* bit better," I said slowly.

"He's a lot better," Uncle Roger said quietly. "His wing is well healed, he's alert and healthy looking. I'd say he's good as new, thanks to you."

"His wing probably isn't very strong yet, though," I said. I looked out the window on my right, studying the fields we were passing.

"I bet you're right. Sammy needs to exercise it to regain his strength."

"How?"

"Well, by flying, mainly."

"If we let him out to fly, will he come back?"

"I can't see it."

I was silent for a moment. I thought of Sammy's bright eyes and his silly squawking voice and the way he tilted his head when he looked at me.

My throat started to hurt.

When I found my voice again, my words came out small and sad. "Can't I keep him as a pet?"

It was Uncle Roger's turn to say nothing, but I could see he was thinking. At last, he said, "I guess that should be your decision, Ellie. Give it some thought for a day or two and let me know what you decide."

I nodded, though I was thinking I could have gone ahead and told him right then and there. Sammy was my bird and I was keeping him, and that was all there was to it.

"Well, here we are."

I was startled to find that we were in the middle of Weybolt. I'd been thinking so hard about Sammy that I hadn't realized it when Uncle Roger turned onto the road that runs through the middle of town. I hadn't even noticed the water tower standing guard over the place.

"I've got a few errands to run," Uncle Roger told me as he pulled up in front of the general store. "But I don't suppose you're too interested in farm equipment or feed supplies. Why don't you go ahead and have a look around in here and I'll meet up with you when I'm finished."

I said okay and got out of the car, but I hesitated once I'd shut the door. Uncle Roger didn't seem to notice. He backed up, gave me a little wave and drove off down the street, leaving me alone, standing on the sidewalk.

A queasy feeling crept into my stomach, and I'd just made up my mind to sit down on the curb and wait for Uncle Roger to come back when I heard someone speak behind me.

"Well, well! If it isn't Miss Ellie! Have you come into Weybolt all on your own today?"

I turned to see Wendell Fletcher standing in the doorway.

"Hello, Mr. Fletcher," I said. "I came with Uncle Roger, but he had to go to a few places."

"That explains why you don't have a car with you," he said, as if he really thought I might be driving a car around the countryside. "But what are you doing out there? Come on away in. And call me Wendell! Everyone hereabouts does."

I accepted the oddly-worded invitation and went in. The queasiness in my tummy was disappearing already. It was occurring to me that I could wander up and down the aisles and look at all the things I'd had to hurry by when I'd been with Grandma.

And then my thoughts got interrupted with a surprise. I had just taken a couple of steps down one aisle when Wendell called me back.

"I see here that you have a two-dollar credit on your account," he said.

I stared at him while the words and meaning came together in my head. Then I told him it must be a mistake.

"No mistake." He turned a large black book around and pointed to the top of a new page. Sure enough, there was my name—Ellie Stewart—written on the first line, and right below it appeared *Credit: $2.00*.

"I reckon someone opened up an account for you," Wendell said, like he didn't know perfectly well exactly how this had come about and could only make an educated guess on the matter.

"My Uncle Roger," I said.

"Could be. Could be. All I can say for sure is that there's a credit here and it's yours." Wendell glanced over as the door creaked open and a couple of women came in. "Mornin', ladies," he said. Then he looked back at me and tapped the page he'd shown me. "Anyway, just keep this in mind while you're meandering about, hear?"

I told him I would and left the counter feeling almost dazed. Two whole dollars! It was incredible wealth—more money than I'd ever dreamed of having. Daddy sometimes gave me a nickel, and once in a while even a dime, but that was about the extent of any riches I'd had before.

For the first while, I wandered about feeling overwhelmed by the vast selection of goods for sale. There were so many things to tempt me—from beautiful bolts of fabric to a wide selection of toys. And, of course, there was candy! Large glass jars stood in a brightly colored line, offering penny candy, peppermint sticks, licorice whips, jawbreakers, and more. Just the sight of them was enough to make your mouth water.

Even though the candies looked and smelled so good, I made up my mind almost right away that I wasn't going to spend any of my credit on them. If I did, they'd be gone in a few moments and I'd have nothing left to show for what I'd spent. I was only going to buy things that I could keep and treasure for always. Things to remember my Uncle Roger by.

That was the exact second when I realized that I was going to miss Uncle Roger when I left. It was a bit of a shock when it hit me, because it wasn't that long ago I'd been sure that there'd never be one single thing I'd miss about this place when Daddy finally came to fetch me back home.

As I stood there, I wondered whether I'd ever see Uncle Roger again after this summer. The thought that I might not made me so sad that for a moment all the excitement over my shopping adventure faded away.

"Anything I can help you find?"

I turned to find Wendell standing next to me. I hadn't even noticed him coming over.

"I want to buy something for my Uncle Roger," I said. The words surprised me.

"Do you now? Well, let's see." Wendell scratched his head. "I happen to know that your uncle is crazy about Coca Cola. Just loves the stuff."

"I was thinking about something he could keep," I said.

"Something to keep, huh? I see." He took a bit longer this time, but then his face lit up and he smiled. "I've got just the thing! Roger loves detective books and there's a brand new one just in. He hasn't even seen it yet."

I followed him to the display rack of books and magazines. He handed me a paperback with a price tag of twenty cents on it. I looked it over. The cover had a picture of a man looking over his shoulder in a dark alley. I decided it was probably pretty exciting.

"Thanks!" I said. "This will be great."

"And what about you, Ellie? I'm pretty sure that whoever put that credit there for you wanted you to get yourself something nice, too."

"I will," I said, "but first I need to get something for my daddy. He'll be coming to get me pretty soon but I want to get him a present for his birthday in September."

I found just the thing in a section where there were a lot of goods just for men on display. There were razors and combs in special cases and boot polish and such, but what caught my eye was a round container labeled *Scented Shaving Soap*. It smelled like our cedar bush back home and Daddy is always saying how nice that smells. I thought he'd sure like to have his face smell the same.

After I put it with the book, I wandered around again but the excitement of having presents to give to Daddy and Uncle Roger kind of took away the fun of shopping for me. That was when I thought maybe I should get something for Grandma. I looked here and there and finally came upon a folding fan with delicate orange flowers painted on it. Grandma is always fanning herself with a paper or piece of cardboard, or even her hand. As soon as I saw the fan I knew it was the perfect thing to get for her.

It was strange how happy it made me to take that fan over to the counter and put it with the book for Uncle Roger and the fancy shaving soap for Daddy.

"Got yourself a fan, did you?" Wendell asked.

"It's for my grandmother," I told him. He nodded and smiled and told me I'd best be finding something for myself before it was too late.

That reminded me that Uncle Roger should be along soon, but it was okay because I knew what I wanted by then. It was a bracelet of brightly colored beads, one of the prettiest I'd ever seen. I fetched it to the counter and asked could Wendell go ahead and wrap it all in brown paper so no one could see what was in it?

He did that and tied it with a string. Then he told me I still had a credit of ninety-three cents but I said he could go ahead and put it on Uncle Roger's page in his book. I was pretty sure I wasn't going to be back to shop again, and even if I was, it seemed greedy to think of buying more things after all my shopping that day.

Twenty

Uncle Roger showed up for me not long afterward. He chatted with Wendell for a bit, and then it was time for us to head back home. He started up the truck again and we drove along past farms that were starting to look more familiar.

When we got to Grandma's place, he didn't turn in at the driveway. I felt nervous when we just kept on past it, because I could picture Grandma at the window, seeing us go by. I knew it would make her angry, though I didn't know why.

Soon as Uncle Roger turned the truck off the road, I realized where we were going. A small graveyard stretched out to our left with a dozen or more rows of stones standing at attention. Some of the gravestones had flowers hugging up to them but most of them were bare or had scrawny little bushes on either side.

"I thought you might want to see where your ma was laid to rest," Uncle Roger said as the truck settled to a stop.

I pulled the handle, swung the door open and stepped out without speaking. Uncle Roger hadn't moved. I paused and looked back at him.

"Over yonder," he said, pointing. "I'll join you after a bit."

My knees had gone wobbly but I managed my way along the rows until I saw the inscription.

Stewart (Acklebee)

Margaret Jean

July 17, 1920—June 04, 1944

It was strange, seeing my birth date carved there like an accusation. I stood for a few minutes, staring at the words, trying to take in the idea that my mother's body was in the ground underneath the spot I was standing. It was the closest I'd ever get to her but it didn't seem like she was there at all.

I'd have thought being at her grave would have made me sad, but it didn't. In fact, I really didn't feel much of anything. Except maybe the emptiness of her place in me—which was suddenly more noticeable.

"Funny the things you think of sometimes."

Uncle Roger's voice startled me a little. I turned to face him, pulling my drifting thoughts to what he was saying.

"I was just remembering how your ma had chicken-pox when she was fourteen. I teased her a good bit about having a little kids' illness at that age. She just laughed it off. Said whatever got her out of doing sums was okay with her. She was never all that fond of school—especially arithmetic." He sank down onto the ground near the stone then. I sat myself down beside him.

"You look like her, you know."

That surprised me more than anything he could have said. The few pictures we had of her backed up what I'd heard my whole life, that my mother had been beautiful. And, as gangly and skinny as I was, I couldn't imagine anyone ever thinking I looked like her.

"You really do," Uncle Roger said, as though he could read my mind. "If I showed you pictures of her at your age, you'd see it. I imagine you'll grow up to look a lot like her too."

"Maybe then Grandma will be able to stand the sight of me," I blurted.

Uncle Roger smiled and shook his head. "I think probably your grandmother finds it hard to look at you *because* you remind her so much of Maggie."

"Grandma says I killed my mother—that Daddy and I did."

He didn't answer right off. Instead, he dropped back onto an elbow and then, after a bit, straight out flat on his back, hands folded under his head.

"Your grandmother has a big load to carry around," he said at last.

"Because my mother died?"

"Well, that's part of it, but it's actually a small part, I'd say. You see, Ellie, when your mom and dad got married, it made your grandma bitter. She'd always been a sort of hard woman, toughened by too many disappointments, I suppose. But this was different.

"She knew how to handle crop failure and hunger, years of poverty, times of sickness and hardship. But she didn't know how to deal with the kind of betrayal she felt when Maggie ran off. It broke her heart, and the only way she knew how to handle it was to close herself off from the hurt."

He fell silent then. I lay down at his side and waited, sure there was more. The sun warmed me and made me lazy. After a bit, he picked up like he'd never paused.

"Some letters came from Maggie but your grandma refused to read them. She burned them in the stove and said she had no daughter. Then the day came when Sheriff Danyluk came to the door holding his hat and saying that Maggie was dead."

"The day I was born," I said.

"The same day," he agreed. "Grandma had been ironing just before he came, and after he delivered the news, she got up and went back to it. Picked up that iron and started in on the shirts like pressing them was the most important thing in the whole world. Faster and faster she went, ironing like a madwoman, until Pa up and took hold of her and pulled her away.

"She let out a long, terrible moan then. I can hear it still. But I never saw her shed a tear or heard another sound of grief from her. It's how she deals with things—maybe the only way she *can*. She just swallows it all down and waits for it to turn cold and hard inside her.

"I know the things your grandmother had said—things like Maggie was dead to her—must have haunted her. Maybe it seemed to her that she'd brought it all to pass somehow, as if her words and thoughts had that kind of power. And even with all of that weighing on her, she held it all in. Not a tear."

Twenty-one

It didn't make any kind of sense that I could understand. Even though Grandma made it clear every chance she got that she didn't want me there, it seemed she was angry if I went anywhere for the day.

The day after I'd been to town with Uncle Roger, she gave me all the worst chores to do, starting off with cleaning the outhouse. I sprinkled lye down the holes and scrubbed the wooden surface you sit on, but that didn't satisfy Grandma. She sent me back out to scrub the floor with a brush. All the time I was in there, flies buzzed around my face, trying to land. I shooed them away frantically, knowing full well where they'd just been.

When I finished that, she told me to take the

carpets out to beat them. Some of them were heavy and I could barely get them up over the clothesline. I guess Grandma would have helped if I'd asked, but I couldn't bring myself to do that.

By the time I finished banging on them with the broom, my throat and eyes were dry and burning from the clouds of dust. I went to the pump-house to get a cold drink of water and to rinse the dirt off my face and get the scratchy feeling out of my eyes.

My arms were sore, too. No matter how long you beat on a carpet, you never get to the end of the dirt in it. I was half surprised that Grandma didn't come out afterward, pick up that broom, and start pounding away—just to make it look like I didn't do a good job.

I went back into the house once I got the grit out of my eyes. Grandma was sitting at the kitchen table, cutting up vegetables for a pot of stew. I told her I was finished.

"Good," she said without glancing toward me or missing a beat in the rhythm of her chopping.

"Do you want me to scrub the floors before I bring the rugs back in?" I asked, when I could find my voice again. I don't know where *that* came from—goodness knows it was the last thing I wanted to do with my arms near about to fall off.

"The floors are done," she said.

So. While I'd been working myself to a frazzle outside, Grandma had been just as busy inside.

I went back outside and began struggling with the rugs, but Uncle Roger came along for his lunch, and he insisted on carrying them all back in and putting them in place. I thanked him and he tweaked my nose, which made a lump come into my throat. Daddy does that sometimes.

"You give any thought to our talk about Sammy yesterday?" he asked as we reached the door.

"Yes." I looked away. "I decided I'm going to keep him. Is that okay?"

"It's all right with me," Uncle Roger said. "You'll need to explain it to Sammy, though, so he knows what's going on."

"Okay," I said, wondering how you explain something to a magpie.

"I'll help you," Uncle Roger added. "How about we have a talk with him after lunch?"

I agreed, though I didn't see why I needed Uncle Roger with me to tell my bird I was keeping him.

As soon as lunch was over with, Uncle Roger told

Grandma we had something to take care of, and he asked if she could excuse me from the dishes for this one time.

"Go," Grandma said with a shrug. "She worked hard all morning."

"Sounds like Grandma appreciates all the help you give her," he said as we neared the shed. I didn't answer, because I was trying to think about what to say to Sammy.

"Ree! REE! REE!" he screeched as soon as we walked inside.

"Hi, Sammy," I said. Then I stood there, not sure how to start. I glanced at Uncle Roger, and he seemed to realize I needed a bit of help.

"Sammy? Ellie came to give you some good news," he said.

I hesitated, then leaned over and spoke very softly to Uncle Roger. "I don't know for sure if it's good news to *him*," I said.

"Oh? Why not?"

"Well, you know...because he might rather be free to fly around and stuff."

"Ah! You know, I think you're right."

I stood there, looking at Sammy and thinking about how small that cage was for a bird that was used to the whole outdoors to play in. And I knew I couldn't keep him there, trapped.

"I guess I changed my mind," I said. "Sammy needs to go back where he belongs." Uncle Roger nodded and didn't look even a little bit surprised.

"You know what, Ellie? I bet you think you're going to feel real sad to let him go, but I don't think you will."

"You don't?"

"When you're ready, we can find out."

I took a big breath, shoved my shoulders back, and said I was ready right then and there. So Uncle Roger carried the cage outside and over to the edge of the field. He sat it on the ground and stepped back a bit.

I walked up to the cage and leaned in close. *"Ree! Ree!"* said Sammy. His dark eyes were darting around and he started to hop up and down. I think he was excited.

"Sammy, it's time for you to go back to your own home," I said. "I'm going to miss you—a lot, but I know you wouldn't be happy staying in this old cage."

I noticed my throat was feeling a bit strange then, so I thought it might be a good idea for me to stop talking and just go ahead and get it over with. I reached down, unlatched the door, and swung it open.

Sammy was completely still for a few seconds. He stared at the open cage door and then lifted his head to look at me, as if he was asking me a question.

"That's right," I said. "You're free now. Go on."

He didn't need any more persuasion than that. Sammy stepped forward and out. Then he hopped a few feet away and shook his wings as if they were dusty and he was clearing them off. He pecked at the ground a few times and hopped about a bit more. Then he spread his wings, opening them more and more until they were fully stretched out at his sides.

I found I was holding my breath, watching and hoping so hard that he would be able to fly. Uncle Roger had warned me right from the start that it was possible Sammy might never be able to fly again. In that case I could have kept him, but I suddenly didn't want to. My whole heart wanted to see him rise up into the air and fly away.

And that's exactly what he did.

I stood very still, watching as he lifted off, flew a few feet, landed, and then repeated the whole process. It was on the fourth try that he stayed in the air, going higher and higher, his wings full of wind and pride.

I felt a tear escape and run down my face, but it wasn't a sad tear. Uncle Roger's hand landed on my shoulder and stayed there.

It came into my head that I should tell him he was right and that I felt much, much happier letting Sammy go than I would have felt keeping him in that cage.

I didn't, but that was because I knew I didn't have to.

Twenty-two

Uncle Roger never seems to forget anything. You might think he's forgotten, but then he brings it up or does something that tells you different.

It was four days after I'd let Sammy go, and we were all sitting at the table having our dinner. Grandma was scowling at me through the meal. I think she was cross because my knife was making screeching sounds on the plate when I was trying to cut my meat but I didn't know how to cut it without making any noise.

Then Uncle Roger turned to Grandma and said something that proves he has a good memory but bad timing.

"Say!" His voice sounded like the idea had just popped into his head that very second, but I knew it hadn't. "It's been the longest while since you made ice cream."

Grandma's fork stopped halfway to her mouth. She looked at Uncle Roger like he'd just suggested she go out and rob a bank or something.

"I betcha Ellie here would love it," he went on. "Be no trouble at all to fetch home some ice next time I'm in town."

"I have other things to do," Grandma said. Then she looked at me accusingly, as if to say she knew perfectly well that I was behind the whole idea, before going back to her food.

"You ever see how ice cream is made, Ellie?" Uncle Roger asked me.

I shook my head and wished he'd just drop it.

"It's a lot of work, let me tell you," he said. "I used to think my arm was going to fall right off turning the handle. Might be too hard for a little girl like you anyway."

"I'm a lot stronger than I look," I said without thinking. I wanted to grab the words back so Grandma wouldn't think I was campaigning for this darned ice cream along with Uncle Roger.

Grandma pushed her chair back suddenly, scraping it along the floor. She stood and went to the stove where the kettle was heating water for the dishes. Only, she didn't pick up the kettle or do anything else. She just stood there with her back to us.

After Uncle Roger and I had finished eating, Grandma sent me to bring in a line of clothes that she'd hung out earlier. She did the dishes by herself. Then she said I should go to my room and be quiet for a change.

I felt bad for Uncle Roger because I knew he wanted things to be one way, only they were another way altogether. There wasn't a thing I could do to change that, either. I might have started to understand why Grandma acted the way she did, but it wasn't in my power to do anything about it.

❖

In spite of what Grandma had told him, Uncle Roger did bring ice back from town the next time he went. Fact is, I think he made up an excuse to go, just so he could get that ice and prove to me that my grandmother cared for me enough to make me ice cream.

Except, she didn't.

Uncle Roger made a point of telling Grandma to be sure to let him know when she wanted him to grate and chip the ice for her so she could go ahead and make the ice cream. But that never happened. The ice just sat there and melted, slowly making a trail of wet that trickled away. And everything went on just as it had been, chores to do and nothing in the air between my grandma and me except prairie dust and heat and silence.

But then, one night…

I'd been getting ready for bed when a tap came on my door. I went to open it with an uneasy feeling, since no one ever came to say goodnight or read me a story like Daddy does at bedtime at home.

I was surprised to see Grandma standing there, with something yellow draped over her hands.

"You can have this," she said, pushing it toward me, "for your dolls."

"Thank you, Grandma," I said. I was too surprised to say anything else and we just stood there for a moment. Then Grandma turned and went down the hall and into her room. She closed the door without looking back at me.

I closed my door too, and took the blanket to the bed, where I unfolded it. It was a pretty yellow quilt covered with hand-stitched daisies. Then I opened it to its full size and saw that it was a little bit too big for a doll blanket. And there was something familiar about it, too.

I stared at it for a moment and then I remembered the quilt Grandma had made for Marcy's aunt when she had a baby. "I start one whenever I hear news that there will be a new baby," Grandma had told me that day.

My breath caught as a thought came to me. Could Grandma have made this little quilt...*for me*, before I was ever born?

I was sure of it, and I tried several ways to ask Grandma about it. But her answers were as cold and stiff as she was, and they gave away nothing.

❖

Uncle Roger never stopped trying to make things seem cheerful, or at least normal, whenever he was around, which was mostly just at mealtimes. As the crops grew he worked longer and longer days. Lots of times he still hadn't come back to the house before I'd gone to bed at night.

I'd lie there after my prayers were said and think about Daddy coming to get me. Sometimes I could picture it just perfectly, and my heart would be beating with happiness just as if it was really happening. Other times, I couldn't get past knowing it was only in my head, and then I couldn't stop the tears from coming.

But in the daytime, when the sun beat down and made the air shimmer in a way that I could almost *see* his car coming, it started to feel like I was hoping for nothing and he was never going to come back for me.

Now and then panic would rise up in me and squeeze me until I could hardly breathe. One time I tried to recite the Twenty-third Psalm, like Daddy said I should do if I was ever troubled deep inside, but I couldn't seem to get it all out. I started out fine with, "The Lord is my Shepherd, I shall not want…," but by the time I got to the still waters my thoughts had drifted and I had to go back to the beginning and try again.

❖

And then, there he was! Only, after all the ways I'd pictured seeing him come down that driveway, I was in the outhouse when it happened.

I didn't even hear the car's familiar rumble—I guess I must have been daydreaming—so it was a huge surprise when I went to wash my hands and heard voices out in front of the house.

I ran, drying my hands on my shirt as I went. My heart was pounding so hard it felt like it might burst.

I rounded the corner and sure enough, there he was! Daddy! He was talking to Grandma, only looking all around as he spoke. I knew right off he was looking for *me*!

He was already reaching down for me as I got to him, and he swung me up and held me against his chest like he used to when I was smaller. His face went kind of crumply for a second, then he took a deep breath and smiled.

"Did you behave yourself for your grandmother?" he asked.

I was about to say I had (because *I* thought I had) but I couldn't—not with her standing right there. So, instead, I told him I'd done my best but sometimes I forgot and made noise.

"I'm sorry, Grandma," I said after confessing.

"Never mind," she said. "Just go get your things."

She didn't need to say it twice! I was so excited packing that I almost forgot about the presents I had for Uncle Roger and Grandma. As soon as I had my things all tucked safely in my bag I hurried downstairs.

"Grandma," I said, suddenly feeling shy, "I bought this for you."

Grandma looked at the fan like she'd never seen one before. Her wizened old hand shook ever so slightly as she reached out for it. She opened it and fanned herself.

"Thank you, Elizabeth," she said. "This is a very useful gift." Then she folded the fan back up and sat it gently on the hall table.

"You're welcome, Grandma," I said. "And thank you for having me and taking care of me all summer."

"Yes. Thank you, Mother Acklebee," Daddy said. "We sure are obliged to you, me and Ellie. And I mean to send you something for your trouble when I go back to work at the mill.

"No," she said, in just the same tone she'd used when she first said I couldn't stay. It didn't leave any room for discussion.

"Well, I sure do appreciate all you've done for us," Daddy said. "I can't thank you enough for taking care of Ellie."

Then we went and got into the car. I thought Grandma would go back inside the house, but she stood there on the front step, her face just as stiff as always. We stopped by the field where Uncle Roger was working, and I hopped out of the car.

"Don't you be a stranger, now, Ellie," he said.

"I won't, Uncle Roger. And I have something for you." I held the book out to him. His face looked surprised and then his mouth kind of trembled and smiled all at the same time. He dropped down on one knee and gave me a big squeeze. Then he cleared his throat a couple of times and said, "Thank you, Ellie. I sure will enjoy this."

Daddy and Uncle Roger shook hands then, and we started out for home.

We had to go past the farm again after saying goodbye to Uncle Roger and I was surprised, looking in, to see Grandma still there on the step.

The sight of her, standing there, like she was frozen in the doorway, made something strange start up inside me. On the happiest day I'd had since I first came to Weybolt, I suddenly felt very much as if I was about to cry.

"Go back!" I said. Daddy turned to me all startled and I realized I'd yelled. I calmed my voice down and then explained. "I have to tell Grandma something."

He didn't ask why. He just turned the car around, drove back to the house, and let me out.

I ran to her and put my arms around her. "I'll write to you and Uncle Roger, Grandma," I said. "I hope you'll write me back."

She didn't answer, but just before I let go and went back to the car and Daddy, I felt her hand barely touch the top of my head.

It rested there for just a second but I could still feel it much later as Daddy and I headed south, a tail of dust rising up behind the car.

Acknowledgements

I am indebted to the following people, whose support for and confidence in *Tumbleweed Skies* helped make this book a reality:

Gail Winskill, who selected and signed the story, and whose forthrightness and integrity made the business end of our dealings painless. Thank you, Gail.

Ann Featherstone, whose skillful editorial hand gently and lovingly guided the words and story into its present form. I am in awe. Thank you, Ann.

Christie Harkin, who was terrific to work with as she managed the home stretch. Thank you, Christie.

And artist David Jardine, whose beautifully rendered cover image is so perfectly suited to the story's voice. Thank you, David.

Books by Valerie Sherrard

Picture Books
There's a GOLDFISH in my Shoe
There's a COW Under My Bed

Children's Novels
Tumbleweed Skies

Young Adult Novels
Watcher
Three Million Acres of Flame
Speechless
Sarah's Legacy
Sam's Light
KATE

Shelby Belgarden Mysteries:
Searching for Yesterday
Eyes of a Stalker
Hiding in Plain Sight
Chasing Shadows
In Too Deep
Out of the Ashes